Larry Brown's

DIRTY WORK

"A powerful and original work all its own that moves along in short, staccato chapters with indisputably authentic language."

—*The New York Times*

"Not only one of the best books about Vietnam but also one of the most powerful anti-war novels in American literature."

—*Atlanta Journal-Constitution*

"[Brown] has created two fully realized, believable—and often very funny—characters.... No one who reads this book is likely to forget them."

—*Houston Post*

"Stunning power... *Dirty Work* makes the human cost of war achingly real."

—*USA Today*

"A spare and inventive novel."

—*Philadelphia Inquirer*

"Courageous... It's hard to imagine a more powerful effect than the one Brown creates with his attentive, unsparing prose."

—*St Louis Post-Dispatch*

"Lean, powerful and effective."

—*Baltimore Sun*

"Bursts with power and humanity."

—*Chattanooga Times*

"A marvelous book...Brown's swift, intuitive dialogue explodes like a land mine and leaves the reader dizzy with shock."

—*Kansas City Star*

DIRTY WORK

DIRTY

A NOVEL

BY

LARRY BROWN

VINTAGE CONTEMPORARIES

VINTAGE BOOKS

A DIVISION OF RANDOM HOUSE, INC.

NEW YORK

FIRST VINTAGE CONTEMPORARIES EDITION, OCTOBER 1990

 Published in the United States by Vintage Books, a division of Random House, Inc., New York. Originally published in hardcover by Algonquin Books of Chapel Hill in 1989.

Library of Congress Cataloging-in-Publication Data
Brown, Larry, 1951 July 9–
Dirty work: a novel / by Larry Brown.—1st Vintage books ed.
p. cm.—(Vintage contemporaries.)
ISBN 0-679-73049-4
I. Title. II. Series.
PS3552.R6927D5 1990
813′.54—dc20 90-50262
CIP

Manufactured in the United States of America

10 9 8 7 6 5 4

For Daddy, who knew what war does to men.

DIRTY WORK

This the trip I took that day, day they brought Walter in. This what things would of been like if it hadn't been for slave traders about three hundred years ago. If history had been different. If I'd of lived in Africa and had me a son and was a king in my own country:

Boy, go down to the river. Take you a spear and you take you some impala jerky and find you an anthill and then you lay there and be quiet. And I don't care how many bugs get to biting you on the ass, you lay there and listen. And keep them eyes open, don't be going to sleep.

I ain't going out there where them things at, Daddy. Them things might eat me up.

They eating my cows up right now. How come I want you to go down there and watch. Them lions eating too much of my meat. I can't be losing no more cows. They think all they got to do is come up here and get one any time they want it. Got to teach em a lesson.

What kinda lesson you fixing to teach em?

You listen to me now. When I was your age I went out and killed me a lion. Hunted him down. Made him charge. Stuck it right in his throat and killed him.

Aw you always telling me what you did when you was *my* age. I ain't never seen you stick no spear in one.

Don't have to. Done stuck mine. You ain't never stuck you one yet. You gonna have to stick you one before you ever get you any of these maidens. You get it? You got to stick one of them before you get to stick one of these.

Well what if I don't?

What if you don't what?

What if I stick me one of these without sticking one of them? What they gonna do then, huh?

What they gonna do? They gonna take you out yonder and put you in that little kraal and make a woman out of you.

How they gonna do that?

With a knife.

Say what!

What I'm telling you. Now get on. You go down there and you watch them cows.

Well what if I see one? What I gonna do then?

Kill it.

Kill it? With this?

With that. Same one I used.

Aw now. This old rusty thing?

Wouldn't be rusty if you'd clean it up. Put you a good point on it. Didn't used to be rusty. You done left it laying out in the mud the reason it rusty. One of them damn lions get after your little ass you gonna wish you'd kept it sharp.

Them things ain't gonna get after me. They ain't studying me. They after them cows. They ain't wanting me.

How you know what they studying? How you know they ain't studying them a easy meal?

Easy meal? What you mean easy meal?

I mean you gonna be easier to catch than one of them cows. Lion he smart. Lion ain't gonna take no chances less you make him mad. He gonna lay up there and look everything over before he makes up his mind. He ain't gonna pick him no strong young bull with horns. Uh uh. He want some old cow slow and fat won't hurt him. Or some little young fat boy who ain't never done nothing more strenuous with his daddy's spear than jab it up and down in the mud. You think I'm playing with you but I ain't. Lion quiet. Slip up on you before you know it. Slip up on you even when you awake. Put them paws down in that dust one step at a time. Same color as the grass. You don't watch your back, he be behind you. Bite your head one time it's all over with. I seen one jerk a warthog out of a hole one time. Tried to catch em and they run in this hole. Old big lion. Big black mane. Had this hole they run into under this bank. Old lion didn't get upset. Didn't do nothing but lay down on top of that bank. He was waiting, see. Wanted him a easy meal. Old lion he laid there. Looked like he was thinking about taking him a nap. Wasn't even paying attention. Knowed them wart-hogs couldn't stand it. Knowed one of em was gonna have to stick his head out in a minute and see was he gone. He just kept laying there. And directly one of them old warthogs stuck his nose out. Sniffing around there. Ain't nothing dumber than a pig. Old lion he just laid there and looked at him. Got up on his belly and got ready. Old warthog stuck his head out a little further, old lion reached his paw out there a little ways. Warthog was just sniffing around all over the place, looking everywhere but up. Took him about a minute to decide everything was cool, that the old lion had done gone. He stuck his whole head out that hole and that lion reached down and hooked them claws under that chin and snatched his ass out so fast it'd make your head swim. Old warthog didn't weigh but about four hundred pounds. It was all over with then. That what I'm telling you. They do you the same way, only easier. You ain't even got no tushes. Only thing you got is a spear. And one come up on you, and you try to stick it in his throat, and it ain't sharp, won't be nothing left of you for me to find but maybe one of your feet. Now you do like I tell you. You take that rock and you clean it up and put you a good point on it and you go down there and you watch them cows for me. Go on now. Don't want to hear no more backtalk. How you think you gonna be the king one of these days? How you gonna give orders if you ain't never had to take none?

He didn't look like much when they brought him in. I come back when they brought him in, quit taking my trip. Don't see much new blood in here. Had him strapped down on a stretcher. Had him knocked out. Hair was all down in his eyes. Even with that I could see his face.

Most of it had been blowed off and they'd tried to put him another one together. RPG probably. Rocket-propelled grenade. On top of that it looked like somebody had clawed the shit out of it. Had scabs on it. Anyway when they rolled him up next to me, I saw what the load of shit he was toting was. Everybody toting something. Some just tote more than others. I laid there and watched him. Couldn't figure out why I hadn't seen him before. Didn't know if that was all that was wrong with him. Other than his face they wasn't nothing else. Had all his fingers and toes. Thought maybe they's just holding him for the padded room. They took the straps off him, though. Took him off the stretcher and put him on a bed. Didn't have nothing hooked to him. Just to look at him you'd think he was dead. They had trouble moving him cause he was so big. He must've weighed about two fifty.

Old boys that brought him said Brought you some company, Braiden.

I said Misery loves it.

I did the smart thing. I woke up before I opened my eyes. I just laid there, I didn't move. There wasn't room for any more mistakes. So I listened. I said to myself, If you were blind, this is what it would be like.

Total blackness. My head on a pillow. A sheet over me. I had the idea that they were watching me to see if I was really asleep. So I decided to fool them. I decided to lie there with my eyes closed and not move a muscle until I knew exactly where I was and exactly what was going on. I knew if I laid there long enough, somebody would come to see about me. They'd come to check my blood pressure, or my pulse. But they wouldn't know I was awake. And if there were two of them, they'd discuss me. That was what I was hoping for: a discussion about me.

It was hard to keep my eyes closed. I wanted to see where I was. It was easy to tell that I was in a different place. The sounds were different. It was quiet, but there was a television playing. I could hear some asshole in a sitcom saying one-liners and canned laughter playing to it. Mama can sit there and listen to that shit all day. Just sit there and rock, watch that TV. And her old chair creaks. Creak and rock, and rock and creak. All day, and sometimes half the night. Creak rock.

No wonder she wants to die. If all I had to watch was a soap opera or a rerun of "Dallas," I'd be ready to die, too.

Whoever was watching the TV wasn't watching anything good, wherever I was. They were probably watching me. And the first thing I had to do was figure out if I was still strapped down without making it obvious that I was awake.

I decided to do it like there were five brain surgeons watching me. I twitched a little. Gave them a little tremor with my hands there. They could pass that off as a nightmare. They could say He's having a nightmare, man. Look at his REM.

I didn't feel any straps.

Lying there like that, trying to fool them if they were there, it reminded me of the second week at Parris Island, and what one guy did to get out of it. He just didn't get up one morning. He just stayed in his rack with his eyes closed and didn't respond when they turned the lights on and started throwing the shitcans around and slobbering like a bunch of mad dogs. He just laid there. On the top rack. He didn't move a muscle when the drill instructor walked over to him and put his mouth right next to his ear and said Well, loved one. Did you not get enough rest last night? Nobody else said anything. We never said anything where they could hear it. We heard every word he said.

We wish you'd get up with us and go eat some breakfast.

We can just go on ahead and let you arrive at your convenience.

Or should we just send you a tray and let you dine in bed?

Would that be all right with you, loved one?

What did that guy feel when he was lying there that morning, with the lights on bright, with that DI talking in his ear, with his eyes locked shut, and the whole platoon listening? Knowing they were going to take him away, and that he'd never see any of us again?

There weren't any straps on my hands. I swelled my chest as much as I could. No bullshit bullhide on it either.

I don't know what he felt. But he stayed locked like that until two corpsmen came and lifted him out of the rack like a board and put him on a stretcher and strapped him down and wheeled him out the door. He never once moved or opened his eyes. We never saw him again. They probably sent him home with a dishonorable discharge. But that was a long time ago. Damn near twenty years. A man could overcome something like that in twenty years.

Maybe that guy was smarter than me. But I don't like to think about smart along with honor and duty and all that shit, so I quit. You either serve or you don't. I was pretty sure I wasn't strapped down. But I wasn't ready to open my eyes. I wanted to keep them closed and think about Beth. What I wanted was to hear her come to my bed and feel her put her hands on me.

But they couldn't talk to me and tell me what had happened if I was asleep. So I opened my eyes. That was my first mistake.

Knowed he wasn't asleep. Seen his hands twitch. He was laying there listening to everything, trying to figure out where he was. This was the dude that had fucked up them guys down on the third floor the night before. Diva'd done told me about that. And he was big enough to. I started to say something to him then. But I wanted to see how long he'd wait. Wanted to see how much patience he had. Wanted to see how smart he was. Made me grin, just looking at him. Didn't even want to go nowhere then. Had something to entertain me then, instead of that television they leave on all day and night, talking about they detergent and *douche* bags and I don't know what all else. Damn old Rex now, he been eating this here dog food for twenty-seven years, he done lost all his teeth and having to gum it, but that's a hundred and ninety-two for you and me. Shit. Make me sick hearing all that old crap. Try to sell you anything, night and day. If they ain't wiping some baby's ass, they cleaning out they commodes or waxing floors or trying to sell you a new TV so you can watch some more of they shit. Want you to buy a Slim Whitman album. Why don't they sell the Temptations, or Jackie Wilson? Hell, why don't they sell some Otis Redding?

He kept on laying there like he was asleep. Didn't want nobody to know he was awake. I knowed, I could tell. Seen every kind of man they is come in here. Seen every thing that can go wrong with them, too. Just a junk pile, this place. Stick you in here when they can't do nothing else with you. When nobody else don't want you, when your family don't want you, when your mama gone and it ain't nobody else.

This dude didn't fit. Except for his face he was a puzzle to me. Whole world's a puzzle to me, though. Why it's got to be the way it is. I don't think the Lord meant for it to be like this originally. I think things just got out of hand.

He was a bro and he was looking at me. Studying me when I opened my eyes. Like he'd been watching me for a long time just to see how long it would take. Somehow, his eyes smiled. But I had to suck in a big breath when I saw the rest of him.

He didn't have any arms or legs, just nubs. Just like *johnny got his gun*.

He winked at me, long and slow. Said Hey main. What's happening? I just shook my head. I didn't know what was happening. Or what had happened. I felt kind of dizzy, and when I tried to raise up, my head felt like it was spinning. I felt like I didn't have any control over my head. So I eased back down on the pillow.

They'd shot me with some kind of shit, evidently, something that would keep me calm and make me be a good boy. I wondered if maybe I hadn't been a good boy already. I wondered if I'd fucked up. I probably had. I do that pretty frequently. Usually about every day. It's how I get by.

I knew I'd just have to lie there until the shit wore off, whatever it was. It wasn't a bad drug. It was sort of nicely numbing. I looked at the guy again. He had his head turned, watching me. He had a very gentle gaze. Not hostile at all. I asked him reckon what kind of shit they had shot me with and he said probably cat tranquilizer. I thought about it for a second, then told him I bet it would really make your old pussy purr. He got to grinning, and then I got to grinning, too. I felt kind of loopy and loose. But I also wondered how he could be in such good spirits. Finally he said he was just kidding me, but they had given me something to cool me out, no shit. I didn't know what he was talking about and he said I'd been a bad boy and didn't want to go along with the program.

I laid there a minute and wondered what I'd done. I didn't know if I wanted to find out or not. So I didn't ask. I didn't ask that, anyway. I asked a real beauty. Asked him how long he'd been like that.

He said twenty-two years.

I closed my eyes. I tried not to concentrate on him. I tried to concentrate on myself, on my situation, and I tried to remember all the things all the doctors had said. What if the scar tissue in my head did cause seizures? How did they know I couldn't live with it for the rest of my life? Haven't people beat cancer? Survived massive heart attacks, and lived through terrible plane crashes? Sure they have. And they'll do it again, too. Just because you get a death sentence, it doesn't mean you have to die. It all depends on the individual person. Everybody's not made alike. Some people can live through what others can't.

I was scared. You wake up in a place like this, a place you've been trying to avoid for years, and you don't know what's happened, or why you're there . . . it's frightening. And alone. That's the main thing. Alone.

Finally I opened my eyes and looked at him. I told him my name was Walter and that I was from Mississippi. He shook his head and grinned, said his name was Braiden Chaney and that he was from Clarksdale. Said he'd chopped a lot of cotton down at Clarksdale. And he apologized for not being able to shake hands with me.

I didn't know what to say to that. So I just looked at what was left of him. I couldn't quit looking at those four black nubs. His head was peeled slick as an egg. He was kind of like a large baby laid up there on a sheet. But he wasn't a baby. He was about forty-something years old.

I knew I shouldn't get started talking to him. I didn't want to get started talking to anybody. All I wanted was to get back home, away from here. Which here I knew by then was a VA hospital somewhere in the South, probably.

But I knew I had to talk to him. There wasn't any way

to keep from it. I told him I lived at London Hill, and that we used to raise cotton on our place a long time ago. Told him I was an old cottonpicking cottonchopper myself, but that not too many people were growing it now.

He nodded and agreed with me. Said everybody he knew was growing that green stuff now. Said that old shit. Said man there was more money in that old shit than a man could shake a stick at. He said he had some friends, and then his eyes went to moving around in his head. He lowered his voice and said he'd give me something but that we had to wait for dark.

I didn't know if he was serious or not. I asked him did he mean wacky tobaccy. Left-handed cigarettes. Boo-shit-tea.

That will make you slap your pappy down, he said. He was grinning like a fiend by then. But it looked like he only had about six or seven teeth scattered around in his mouth. From somebody else having to brush his teeth for him, I figured.

We didn't talk for a while after that. I knew one thing would lead to another. It always does. I wondered what could have eaten him up like that, but I knew. A machine gun, or a mine. Or hell, maybe a claymore. Maybe even one of our own claymores. They loved to slip up on sleeping lookouts and take some white paint and paint the side that said FRONT TOWARD ENEMY white and turn it around and wake the lookouts up, so they'd pull the string and shoot themselves in the face with about three pounds of buckshot.

But I didn't want to talk about that. Or rockets, or machine guns, or fragmentation grenades, or exploding beer cans. Those were the last things in the world I wanted to talk about. I just stayed there and didn't say anything for a while. But he never stopped watching me.

My man didn't want to talk, I understood that. It was cool. Inside he was probably shaking like a cat shitting peach pits. Hell, come in here, wake up like a duck in a different world quacking. Don't know nobody. I don't think he even knowed his face was all clawed up. Somebody with some fingernails had laid into him. What it looked like. And they had probably give him so much dope since he was so big his mind wasn't right yet. So I knew to lay back, just have patience.

Old patience hard after this long, though. Old patience done flew out the window after this long. Lay in here and lay in here and lay in here. Have to watch all that pussy on TV. Miss America. "Days Of Our Lives."

Oh Lance, won't you please come over here and sniff of my magnificent breasts?

Oh Lance, I believe you is bringing me to the brink of a tremendous organism. Yes. Oh, Lance, dolling, oh, oh, oh no don't put the *root* to me!

Get you some this here love bone.

Wait a minute now, Lance!

You know you been asking for it.

Lance, you get that thing away from me now, that's a *weapon*. Let's talk this thing over.

Shoot. Don't need that. Takes too long just thinking about it. I need to invent me something like a radio show. Go on broadcast every night. Be on FM and be a voice in the little blue lights. Be nice to do something for kids. Have some late show they could stay up and listen to. Have pajamas on and stuff. Cowboy hats. I'da loved to had me some kids. Little old naked babies you could wash in the tub and stuff. Make you so happy you wouldn't know what to do. Little black asses running around all over the house. Wonder if the Lord made the black man at midnight. We know You love us. We love You, too. I mean, six, seven thousand years from now . . . won't make no difference, will it? Everybody gonna be so mixed up by then that far in the future that they all gonna be the same color by then, ain't they? Whyn't You set me down here five or six thousand years later? They won't even have no damn guns by then probably. And I could move on me some one-sixteenth Polynesian milkmaid from Hamburg with a uncle in New York whose brother was a Jewish guy. Naw, I know, can't do it. Got to keep us all separated. But how come they ain't a word in black language for them bad as they word in white language for us? Why didn't we think us up a bunch of good words instead of picking all their damn cotton? We wasted about two hundred years picking fucking cotton.

I know. I'm a sinner. I have lustuous thoughts every day. Cause they show it on TV. Bob Barker's got them girls on the tube all the time. Who is that . . . that Janet Pennerton? Naw, that other one. That poody woody one. She is so fine. One of em done had a baby now she don't look as fine. What'd I do with that *National Enquirer* that had that picture of her in it? I never did finish reading that story about that little space-boy come in them people's window had them two little space-puppydogs with helmets on sticking out his butthole anyway. Hell they done got it over there. All the way across the room. I guess the damn nurses been reading it. Well shit. Muse yo self. Spect yo self. Wawa wawa wa.

All right, motherfucker, where's the damn Percy Sledge album? Getting tired of this shit. Y'all gonna give away *two million dollars* or you gonna show the damn movie? Why hell I done seen that one three times. That's the guy that gets all them kids in that boat and then rows em all the way across the Pacific Ocean with two stale crackers to eat the whole way over there. I don't want to see that shit no more. That's bad as that one the other night where this guy had this rare disease, one of them rare disease movies. Why don't y'all put something good on? Have to watch some old fat-ass white lady trying to win her a car or something. Trip to Mexico. Won't put on nobody good like Humphrey Bogart rolling them little steel balls around in his hand. Old Humphrey could get the damn women. Had them women crawling all over him. He was so swab and debonair with them women. I liked the one where he was pulling old Katherine Hepburn around in that boat and got them leeches on him and got the heebie-jeebies every time she pulled one off. They don't make movies like that no more. If you dumbass Casual Company rejects over there had any culture you'd turn it over there on some National Geographic stuff or something educational. Naw I'm a trump I'm a spade naw you broke the widder what is all that shit about anyway. Play poker like y'all some hot-shit gamblers till it drives me up the wall and bet damn nickels. Bring it over here sometime if you want to gamble. I maybe can't deal but by God I can play if somebody'd hold the cards for me. I got the money. Naw. Y'all can't communicate with me.

Y'all ain't stuck in here. Y'all just got to come in here in the daytime and make a bunch of noise and fuck up my movie watching. Y'all done just smoked too much dope or wrecked your car cause of some dope dependency from some dope habit you picked up overseas and ain't never come down yet. Ain't never smoked no dope cause you had to. You just don't know what it is. Fear. Help you get you some heightened awareness. You know your ass can be blowed off any second, you choose the heightened *perception*. When that trip wire's like a hair, and you on your knees, and everybody behind you trying to be silent and black and invisible, and they don't take a step till *you* say that next six inches is clear. . . .

You boys don't know what it was like. Y'all didn't grow up with the threat of a war hanging over your head. They was drafting then. Couldn't just worry about pussy. Had to worry about going to *war* and getting your *ass* shot *off*. Especially if your ass was black as mine. Yeah. Aw yeah, y'all went out and trained, I know. But you ain't got that threat over you. My mama, Lord, she cried, just took on something awful. Wasn't never gonna see her baby again. Got down on her knees and begged You not to take me. Couldn't stand to see me go. Closer to time it got, more she cried. Every night.

What'd she think, reckon? You's gonna step down between me and the U.S. Government? She prayed enough for it, didn't she? Never saw a woman so heartsick. Looked good then, didn't I, Lord? Two hundred and nineteen pounds of blood and bone and muscle. That old woman raised me on peas and biscuits. Go home that's what she'd feed me. Tell me to eat. Last time I left I know I was laying in there in my bed and I woke up just before it was daylight. Light was on in the kitchen, and I could smell her cooking biscuits. Wasn't nothing but a little old shack. I was gonna build her something better later. I woke up, just wide awake. I was leaving that day. Boarding a plane at Memphis, going for orientation and weapons fire before we jumped off. What we called jumping off. Jumping off the world. I had all that in head of me and I woke up in my mama's house with her cooking biscuits for me. Smelled the same way every morning. Always smelled the same. She never woke me. Didn't have to. Biscuits woke me. I heard her tell people, That child can smell them biscuits in his sleep and when he smells em he wakes up. My mama was so good to me.

I laid in there that morning. Had my uniform hanging up in there. Soldier of the most powerful nation in the world. And all I could think was Why, you know, why? I didn't even understand the whole thing. Just went cause it was my duty. I'm sure there was plenty who went didn't understand the whole thing. Just went cause it was their duty. This my country, I'm gonna fight for my country. Sentiment was strong for God and Country, young boys, listen up. Everybody's daddy had been in World War II. Some daddies, anyway. Now they telling us we won't never be in another one like that one again. That one taught us a lesson. We ain't having no more futile wars. Till we have one in the Middle East. Or down in Nicaragua.

Ain't no need in having a war lessen they just bomb

the hell out of you like Pearl Harbor or something. Then all you can do is just bomb the shit out of them right back, and fight, and get a whole bunch of people killed and finally not accomplish a goddamn thing except get your economy ruined forty years later.

Everything just pisses me off. The world gets worse all the time. Had one man one time that would have stopped it. Of course they had to kill him. And then things just went to shit. I don't know what they want to watch this crap like "The Love Connection" for. If all these people so attractive and not married why ain't they out legging down off TV? They seem like they had a good time, though. I guess I sort of like "The Love Connection." I like old Chuck Woodery. But half the time these motherfuckers'll let you get halfway through a program and then switch channels. Fraid they might miss something else. That morning I woke up in my mama's house was the last morning I was whole, and with her. I'd shined my shoes the night before. Me and her had watched some old movie on TV. I'd brought us home a sixpack of Miller. Loved her a cold beer, now. She drank two and I drank three. It was old Jimmy Stewart in something. He was in the Civil War. And he got shot, and he had this beautiful horse, and his arm was almost blowed off, and this doctor said he couldn't save his arm but saw that horse he was riding and remarked over what a fine animal it was. This guy was like a low-down motherfucker on the battlefield of life. Couldn't save his arm, see, just couldn't save it. Then he seen old Silver over there. And old Jimmy

Stewart told him, Doc, if you'll save my leg, arm, whatever it was, you can have that horse. Well the old Doc decided he might could save it then. What I'd love to seen after he got through fixing old Jimmy Stewart's arm was about four corporals come in there and get him and march him out to a wall and shoot the sumbitch full of holes. But old Jimmy never did write home again and his mama thought he was dead and finally President Lincoln got him in his office and told him he'd better write his mama if he knew what was good for him. Bunch of years later they (after they got happily reunited) found his old horse pulling a coal wagon in Kansas City or somewhere and bought him back for like five bucks. They was gonna keep him in a warm barn and all for the rest of his life. It was a real heartwarming story. It was a happily ever after.

What you got to do is stay up late at night and check your *TV Guide* for this good stuff. You'll maybe see it once in the next fifty years. I done seen it. Just can't remember the name of it.

But me and Mama had a good time that night, watching that movie. We was cooking us some popcorn in between times. She'd run in there and turn the burner on and run back in and set down and I'd run in there and put the popcorn on and she'd run in there and shake it and run back and then I'd run in there and shake it and that way didn't neither of us miss much. And we had butter. REAL butter. Not this fake shit now. My mama still had a churn between her legs every morning.

But it come time to go. That morning it did. She fixed

me some coffee, I was smoking for the first time in front of her. She didn't see me leave from Memphis. She just saw me leave from Clarksdale. Cotton was up. Most of them around us had a pretty good stand. Looked like they's gonna make it good that year. I felt better, finally, looking at it, knowing I wasn't going to have to chop no more of the shit. My little sister was standing out there with us. Old boys I knew from Tunica was taking me to Memphis. They was all out there in the car waiting. One of them times, you know. I didn't have to report until the next morning. We was going to Beale Street that night. But there my mama and them having to tell me goodbye. And what a thing for her, me having to go off to something like that. Ain't no words to say, except the ones everybody thinking about but just don't want to say. Don't die.

What you gonna tell em? You can't do nothing but kiss em and hope they right.

I wish they'd put that other movie back on, that one I seen that time. One where that guy had all his arms and legs blowed off and his face too. That guy talked to Jesus a couple of times. I don't think Jesus ever come and set on his bed like He does mine, though.

I was thinking about Thomas Gandy. He was a little kid who lived right down the road from us when I was a little kid. It was right after they sent my daddy to the pen.

You ever tried to remember the earliest thing you could remember? I mean when you were little and what you were doing? I have. For a long time the earliest thing I could remember was riding on a wagonload of cotton with some little black kids and jumping around in it. But I got hypnotized one day by this girl who was going to school over at Ole Miss and after I came to I got to remembering some stuff that was even earlier than that. It was a long time ago. I saw a man get killed. Well, I didn't really see it. I just saw him after he got killed.

Nobody's ever talked about it to me. Not even my mother. Some things people just don't talk about.

In my mind I put myself about four. Maybe I was five. I don't know. I know Max wasn't born yet.

The thing I remember most is the man lying there in a big pool of blood. It was black. Like he was stuck in the middle of a great big scab that was growing on the ground. I remember us on the porch, just sitting there, looking at him. I know I kept asking Mama something, over and over. I guess it was because I couldn't figure out why that man was just lying in our front yard, not moving.

My daddy killed him over something about my mother, but I don't know what it was. I don't know if this guy was trying to go with her or what.

I think I heard the shot. I don't know where I was. That's what's aggravating about it. Maybe if I'd seen it, I might have been able to understand what it was all about. But I didn't. It's like I just appeared on the porch and saw him lying there. A dog came up and smelled him. I remember that. Then the dog jerked backward and went away.

I know they came and got my daddy that day. They must have. I mean you can't just kill somebody and then hang around the house. When you do something like that, you've got to pay for it. I know. I've had to pay for a lot of things myself.

After they hauled my daddy off to the pen, that left me

and Mama to fend for ourselves, as they say. We had to get our cotton patch through the summer without the weeds taking it and then get it picked in the fall. I don't know how she did it. But I do know how she did it. She got out there with a hoe and worked, all day, every day. Maybe I was five. I can't think. My head's still messed up. Five or six. I helped her. Wait a minute. Max is six years younger than me. Maybe she was pregnant when they took him. I bet that's what it was. Hell. Maybe he freshened her loins the night before he shot that asshole, whoever he was. He must have been an asshole. He must have done something really shitty for my daddy to have to shoot him and go to the pen.

Anyway I was thinking about Thomas Gandy. He was a little bitty kid with glasses and a crew cut. His head looked like a bristle brush, and his glasses could blind you in the sun if he bounced the light on you just right. You'd be throwing your hands up in front of your eyes like the Prince of Darkness was coming in the window. Thomas was a real milquetoast who cuts folks like me's heads open now and makes a lot of money for fixing whatever's wrong with their heads. I think that's why I was thinking about him. I know they're wanting to take a look inside my head. They've been wanting to do that for a good long while now.

Yeah but old Thomas, he didn't always occupy such a lofty position in the world. No sir. At London Hill, Mississippi, a long time ago, he was once forced to *eat* a large piece of dried cowshit and then say it was good and almost say that he'd like some more, please, with sugar on top.

Matt Monroe was a sadistic little bastard when he was six years old and the only thing that's changed about him is he's grown. And there was a time when he worried me a lot. He doesn't worry me now. Now he's as nice to me as he can be. There used to be a school at London Hill and that's where I started. It was a big old white building on a hill. Kids from Paris and Potlockney and DeLay went there, but there weren't very many of us in each class. I didn't know anybody until I started to school. But it didn't take me long to find out I didn't want anything to do with Matt Monroe.

He caught old Thomas Gandy out there in the yard about the third day of school. Miss Lusk, our teacher, had stepped down the hill to the store to get some more milk for the kids. I didn't know what was happening, but Matt turned on Thomas and every eye on the playground turned with him. He backed him around the side of the schoolhouse and down to the fence where Mr. Autry Jordon kept his cows. Then he pulled Thomas Gandy's glasses off. We knew something bad was coming. Thomas Gandy, future brain surgeon, was about to be humiliated. And we were like a bunch of little ghouls getting ready to watch it. One kid went to be a lookout on the corner.

Old Thomas was sort of blinking in the sunlight, slowly. Trying to use the vast resources of his awesome mind to help him.

Matt Monroe peeled off a piece of dried cowshit from

where a cow had hiked her tail against a post and told Thomas Gandy to eat it.

Thomas said he wasn't going to do it. Said he was gonna tell Miss Lusk on him.

Matt Monroe's eyes were too close together and he had long greasy hair that he used either Vitalis or Vaseline on. He weighed about eighty pounds. About forty more than Thomas.

I think Matt said, "You tell Miss Lusk and I'll knock your head off. You whore. You queermouth." That's the kind of child Matt was. He had Thomas backed up against the post by then, and Thomas was doing everything he could to keep that turd out of his mouth. He had his jaws locked. He had his eyes wide open.

Matt told him to open his mouth and close his eyes, and he'd give him a big surprise. And just as he was about to try and jam the cowturd in, Thomas clamped down on his hand like a dog that hadn't eaten in about a week and started gnawing it for all he was worth. He was slobbering a little, like Matt Monroe's hand was the best thing he'd ever tasted. Matt finally got his hand out of Thomas Gandy's mouth and he wasn't happy about it. It was bleeding, and it had little fang marks all over it. Everybody just hushed. It was like seeing Sonny Liston get knocked down by Willie Pep.

Thomas wound up on the ground with Matt on top of him. He let out this big grunt. Matt had his arms pinned, with his knees on his shoulders. He had that old cow-turd right over his mouth. Thomas kept shaking his head.

He set a record for holding his breath that day. He held it until his face turned purple, then black. Then he had to open his mouth to get him a big breath. And the old cowturd went right in there.

People think man is cruel. Hey, what about the *child* of man? There ain't nothing meaner than some little deranged six-year-old sadistic motherfucker loose in a playground. You think a person's got to be grown before he's a maniac? *Shit.*

"Say it's good!" Matt screamed.

"Bood!" sprayed Thomas. "Beal bood!"

"Now say you want some more!"

"Wampfmore!"

I think you'll agree with me when I say that Matt Monroe's mother should have put him in a towsack and drowned him when he was little.

"Please!" Matt shouted.

"PWEESE!"

"With sugar on top!"

Thomas never did put in his request for sugar on his cowshit because he started crying and could only say Shhh, shh, shh after that. I guess Matt thought that was good enough. He let him up and gave him back his glasses. Old Thomas wouldn't even look at us when he left. But he did exactly what he'd told Matt he was going to. He went and told Miss Lusk on him.

She burnt Matt Monroe's ass up. Broke a yardstick on his ass and then grabbed a lightcord and flayed him with that for a while. I laughed out loud. And Matt Monroe saw me. I'm sure Thomas Gandy with his superior brain knew better than to laugh. I didn't.

People don't know what it's like to be poor. I was raised poor. We got our water from a well and we had to carry it to the house in a bucket. I never lived in a house with running water until I was fourteen years old. Instead of turning on an air conditioner we sweated.

When it was real hot, in the middle of the summer, Mama would let me put my bed out on the back porch and sleep out there. You could catch that night wind and hear everything out in the woods calling, crickets and frogs and birds. You could even hear a fox bark once in a while, or coondogs running down in the bottom. You could see our cotton patch down behind the house with the night laying over it, letting it cool down. See the rows in the dark. Lie there in the cool and think about how nice it was to just stay right there and not have to be out in the sun, chopping cotton, sweating, working your ass off. You could even, for a while, forget about people like Matt Monroe. The perverted little bastard.

I'd have to call Matt Monroe trash. There's nothing else to call somebody like him. You could just tell by looking at him that he was trash.

But of course trash is always in the eye of the beholder. I know. There were probably some people who thought we were trash. I know there were people who looked down their noses at us because we were on welfare. That and my daddy being in the pen.

I know people who say, well, I wouldn't be on welfare

and take food stamps or handouts, I've got too much pride. That's fine. Pride is a fine thing to have. The only thing is, you can't eat pride. But you can eat commodity eggs and flour and rice and cheese and butter and powdered milk, and your babies can eat commodity cereal and drink commodity formula and fruit juice and live without pride. Pride ain't worth a damn to a hungry kid who wants something to eat, and if a man says he wouldn't take welfare food when his kids didn't have anything to eat, if he said that, he's lying, and I'd tell him so. I know. My mother swallowed her pride and went every week and got that stuff.

Some people from the welfare office in town came around every week to the post office in London Hill and gave out food to the people on the list. My mother never said anything about it, but I know it hurt her. We had to walk about a mile to get up to the post office from our house. We lived on the south side of what you could call town if it was a town. But it's not. It's just a little community about like a thousand others scattered all over the state. Just a little crossroads up in the hills where somebody a long time ago decided to build a house because it had a creek they could get water out of or there was some good timber to cut. The school's gone now, they tore it down a long time ago. But I can go by there any time I want to and see the spot where Matt Monroe first got me down on the ground.

The welfare people always came on Thursday afternoon at four o'clock. I'd go home from school and my mother would be out in the field, and she'd come in and wash up and get ready. Then we'd leave the house and walk back up to London Hill. The roads were all dirt then, and if somebody came along in a vehicle while we were walking, we'd have to get over on the side of the road where the grass was and walk there until they passed. In the summertime it would be dusty, and the dust they raised would settle on us and you could smell it in your nose like something old and sour.

There was at one time a store that sat in the middle of London Hill, an old store. The tin on the roof had rusted brown a long time before that and the whole thing leaned a little to the left. It had a faded red kerosene tank out front with a pump handle, and old wooden benches that were covered with knife cuts and people's initials where men had sat there year after year and whittled on them, and it had yellow signs with thermometers and ancient Coca-Cola signs tacked all over the front. The screen door was patched with wads of cotton and it had a strip of blue tin in the middle that said Colonial Bread is Good Bread.

I never went in the store much when I was little because I never had any money to spend. Usually the only time I'd go in there was when my mother sent me to the store for Kotex. You ever had to go to the store for Kotex? I have. And it's embarrassing. It'll also get you into trouble with white trash like Matt Monroe if somebody like Matt Monroe is in there when you go in for your Kotex.

I think this was the first time I ever scored any Kotex, without knowing what it was. Mother had called me into the house from whatever I was doing, I don't remember what. She was hiding behind the kitchen door, just her face looking out. Kind of pale and worriedlike.

"I need you to go to the store for me," she said. She had a dollar bill crumpled up in her hand. "I need some Kotex."

"Kotex," I said.

"It's in a blue box," she said. "Don't get the Junior. Get the Super."

"Super."

"And hurry."

"You want me to run, Mama?"

"Yes, honey. Run. Please."

"Can I get me something if there's any left over?"

"Yes, get you a Coke or something, but hurry."

So I hurried. I didn't know what Kotex cost but I was sure it wouldn't cost a dollar. I was hoping it would only cost about ninety cents. I could get a Coke for a dime, that or a big Nehi grape. And it was entirely possible that the Kotex would only cost eighty cents or something like that, so that maybe I could get a Moon Pie to go along with it. All the way up there I was wondering what to get. And I was happy. I wasn't even tired from that mile run. I slowed down when I got close to the store, and there were about seven or eight old men sitting around out front there, spitting and whittling some more wood off the benches. Talking about cows and stuff, I guess.

I didn't know any of those old men and I was shy, too,

so I just looked down at the ground when I walked in between all their legs. Of course they were quiet when I went by. I stepped inside the store and the boards creaked. They sagged in places, and the holes in them were patched with pieces of tin nailed down to the wood. It was dusty and dark and there was a stove in the center of the room with a pipe going up through the ceiling. And behind the counter was the meanest looking old man I'd ever seen. He had white hair and a leathery old face with white whiskers bristling all over it and he had brown stains going down from the corners of his mouth. I knew what his name was. He was Mr. Davis. He had faded blue eyes and his voice sounded like gravel sliding across a washtub.

"Hep you?" he said.

"Yessir," I said. I stepped on up there with my dollar. "I need me some Kotex."

He acted like it insulted him. He gave me a sharp look. He moved out from behind the counter, shuffling in his house shoes. His black pants were baggy and his white shirt was dirty. The Kotex was up on a high shelf and he reached and pulled one down and swatted the dust off it with his hand. I laid my dollar on the counter and waited while he brought it over. Blue box. Kotex Sanitary Napkins. Junior.

He'd already set it down and started back around the counter. I looked at him and he stopped.

"Well," he said. "What else?"

"Super," I said.

"*What?* Speak up, boy, cain't hear you! Damn near deaf!" he screamed. He had one hand cupped behind his ear.

"Super!" I shouted. "Need the Super! She said not get the Junior!"

"Goddang, boy," he said, and he snatched the box off the counter. "Speak up, speak up." He muttered and mumbled while he shuffled back across the room and reached and put it back and got a box of the Supers.

"All right. What else?"

"How much?"

"Sixty cents. Out of a dollar." He'd already picked up the money.

"I want to get something else," I said. He waited while I went over to the drink box. I opened the lid and looked down in it. The drinks were all in glass bottles and they were standing up to their necks in ice cold water. Cokes and Nehis and SunRise Oranges and 7-Ups and Royal Crown Colas and Dr. Peppers all lined up in formations like soldiers. It was hard to decide what I wanted. I settled for a big Nehi grape and closed the lid. I opened it and looked around for the Moon Pies. There was an open box of them on top of the drink case. I got one and carried it and the Nehi back to the counter.

I asked him if I had enough money to get all that but he didn't say anything. He just rang it up and gave me my change. Twenty cents. Two dimes. I thanked him and started out.

"Wait a minute," he said. "Here's you a sack."

"That's okay," I said. "I don't need a sack."

"You better put it in a sack. So everbody won't see it." He kind of mumbled that.

I couldn't really see the logic, but I waited for him to put it in a sack. I dropped my Moon Pie in there, too.

I went out the door and the voices hushed again when I went by. I didn't look at anybody and I kept my head down until I got past them. Then I took a drink of my Nehi and walked straight into Matt Monroe. He was standing there waiting for me. He pulled an ambush on me and I walked straight into it. I think he asked me where I was going. I said I was going home, I was in a hurry.

He wanted to know what I had in that sack. I said nothing, and started around him, sipping on my Nehi. Boy it was good and cold. Delicious. Mean little son of a bitch.

"I know you," he said. "Don't I?"

"I don't know," I said. "I got to go."

"Yeah, I know you," he said, and he caught hold of my shirt. "You the one that was laughing at me when Miss Lusk gave me that whippin'."

"No," I said. "That wasn't me."

"You a lyin' son of a bitch."

I stopped. I had to. I couldn't move.

Let me see how to put this. I enjoyed watching Matt get his ass blistered by Miss Lusk. I enjoyed that. He deserved it. But I'd be lying if I said I didn't enjoy watching Thomas eat the cowturd, too. But part of me also *hated* watching Thomas eat the cowturd. Because I knew that it could very easily have been *me* eating the cowturd. So I should have known not to laugh when Miss Lusk tore his ass up.

I was scared. Scared bad. I'd seen the fear in Thomas Gandy's eyes, and how easily Matt Monroe had thrown him down and gotten on top of him. I was afraid that Matt Monroe was about to do something terrible to me, and I was right.

He drew back his fist and hit me in the nose so hard I couldn't see anything. I turned loose of everything and sat down in the gravel. When I opened my eyes he was drinking my Nehi. He set it down and started in the sack after my Moon Pie. I got up to take it away from him, but the sack ripped, and the blue box of Kotex fell out on the ground. Matt Monroe didn't even look at the Moon Pie. He had eyes only for the box of Kotex. I wiped a little blood away from my nose with the back of my hand and bent over to pick it up.

"Kotex," he said. "*Kotex*," like it was a dirty word.

I'd be lying if I said I wasn't crying a little by then. My nose was hurting so bad I still couldn't hardly see anything. Bleeding pretty bad. I was scared of Matt Monroe. I knew there was nothing I could do about him drinking my Nehi. I knew there was nothing I could do about him eating my Moon Pie. But I knew I had to get that Kotex home in a hurry because my mother was standing behind the kitchen door looking worried about it.

I looked back at the store, knowing what I'd see. All those old men looking at me, watching Matt Monroe take my stuff away from me. And they were. Every one of them was watching to see what I was made of. And they saw. Chickenshit. That's what I was made of.

I picked up my dirty Kotex, and I went on home.

That day, anyway.

I tried to wipe all the blood off my face before I got home so Mama wouldn't see it. I pulled my shirttail out of my pants and tried to wipe it away, but it didn't work. She saw it as soon as I walked in the house. She was still hiding in the kitchen, and she saw it when I handed her the Kotex.

After she did what she had to do in the kitchen, she came storming out from behind the door and grabbed me. She asked me what had happened to me. She was almost screaming, and that scared me worse than Matt Monroe had. I told her a boy named Matt Monroe had taken my stuff away from me and hit me in the nose and that he was a bully and he was too big for me to fight. I guess I was expecting some sympathy. She was the wrong place to look for it.

"What do you mean?" she said. "What do you *mean* letting him run over you like that? What did he say?"

I told her he didn't say anything. He just hit me in the nose and knocked me down.

"And you just *took* it? Without fighting back?"

I was crying and she was shaking me. I know now that she was ashamed of me. Not my father's son. Hell, I was ashamed of myself.

"Did he say anything about your daddy? You tell me. What did he say?"

"He didn't say nothing. He just hit me."

She turned me loose then. I wouldn't look at her. She sat down in a chair. I'll never forget what she told me.

"Boy, I'm gonna tell you something. If you don't take up for yourself in this world, there ain't nobody else that will. If you let him run over you once, he's gonna run over you again. The next time he sees you, he's gonna run over you. Cause now he knows he can. So you got to teach him right now that he can't. Either now or the next time, it don't matter. Is he bigger than you?"

I said Yesm, a lot bigger.

"Well," she said, and she got up like it was all settled. "I guess you gonna have to just pick you up a stick, ain't you?"

I didn't say anything.

"Ain't you?"

Yesm.

"Don't you never let nobody say anything about your daddy. You hear me? I don't care what you have to do. Just don't you let it happen."

That was the end of that conversation.

I went to bed that night and thought about it. I thought about watching Thomas Gandy and wondering about how he felt when Matt Monroe got him down on the ground and shoved that shit in his mouth. And I knew then that he'd felt just like I did right then. Awful.

I didn't want to go to school the next day. I laid in the bed and moaned and groaned for a while and made out like I was sick, but one smack of her hand on my little ass got me going in a hurry. And she watched me walk up the road until I was out of sight.

Picture it if you can. Ten minutes before eight and all of them waiting for you on top of the hill at the schoolhouse, Matt Monroe out in front. You with your little books and tablets, trying to get inside the door before they see you. But of course they've already seen you, and they move forward in a group to surround you. There, in the crowd of grinning faces, you spot a former friendly face that has turned rabid and reverted with the rest of them through fear: the smiling, bland, four-eyed face of Thomas Gandy, future brain surgeon.

"Here he comes," Matt Monroe said. "The Kotex Kid."

He blocked the steps with his body and the rest of them formed a subtle flanking maneuver, barring my way.

Nobody else will. Let him run over you once, he's gonna run over you again. Next time he sees you. Cause now he knows he can.

I think it was at that moment that I realized that the world was not always a nice place to live. And there were no sticks at all. Not one.

"Y'all let me by," I said. I'm sure my voice was small and thin and very whiney.

"What'sa matter?" Matt Monroe said. "You got to go in and git you some Kotex?"

The girls all giggled, the little darlings. I should have known he'd told everybody.

Then there came the most wonderful sound I'd ever

heard: the bell. And like magic Miss Lusk appeared at the top of the stairs. She told us it was time to get inside. Matt Monroe smiled. They all smiled.

"Recess," he said. Who knows what fear lurks in the hearts of children?

I watched that clock like a man getting ready to be stood up against a wall and shot. Each time I looked over at Matt Monroe, he'd be looking at me and grinning. He'd mouth the words silently with his lips, sweetly. *Kotex Kid.* I knew I had to do one of two things. Stay inside at recess and fake being sick, or rush outside ahead of everybody and find a stick. I didn't know what he was going to do to me but I knew that I would almost certainly not like whatever it was.

The buzzer rang at ten o'clock sharp and all the kids left their books and went outside. I stayed in my seat and watched. Matt Monroe was the last one out. He stood in the doorway and looked at me. He pantomined it. *Kotex Kid.*

"Walter?" It was Miss Lusk. She was sitting at her desk reading a magazine. "Go outside and play."

I immediately got a sick look on my face. I tried to will myself into a fever. She was no dumber than my mother.

"I don't want to go outside, Miss Lusk," I said. "I don't feel good."

She put her magazine down.

"Are you sick?"

"I just don't feel good."

"Do you have fever?"

"I don't know. I may have."

She got up and came back there and laid the back of her hand against my cool clammy forehead.

"You don't have fever," she said. "Now go on outside and play with them. The fresh air will make you feel better."

You didn't argue with Miss Lusk. She didn't put up with any foolishness. But she didn't know what she was sending me out into. And I couldn't tell her. There was still a shred of dignity that kept me from using that most craven of cowardly children's acts of self-preservation, hiding behind the teacher's skirts. I couldn't do that. I was a coward, and I knew it, but I couldn't do that. So I went out to meet what was waiting for me.

They were right outside the steps. The whole first grade. Waiting for me.

They gave me enough room to step into the midst of them and then they closed back around me. Matt Monroe was instantly up in my face.

"What you trying to do, chickenshit, hide behind Miss Lusk's skirts?"

"Leave me alone, Matt," I said.

"Leave me alone, Matt," he whined. He cocked his head. "You come on around here."

Matt Monroe had some black rotten teeth in his mouth and his breath smelled like something that had been dead out in the woods for about a week. He had thick lips and long downy hair all over his chin. He had one big brown wart right in the middle of his chin with one long black hair growing out of it.

"Your mama wears Kotex," he said. "On her head."

I didn't say anything.

"I wish I had me a shirt like that," he said. "One to shit on and one to cover it up with."

I think it's probably safe to say that Matt Monroe did not grow up in a Christian home.

"Queer. You dickface."

I still hadn't said anything and I could tell they were disappointed. And for some reason, they backed off and left me alone. Then I turned around and saw Miss Lusk standing behind us, holding out her hand, saying, "I wonder if it's going to rain?"

My mother wanted to know what happened at school that day when I got home.

"Nothing," I said.

"Did that boy say anything to you?"

"Nome."

"You sure?"

"Yesm."

"Don't worry. He will."

That's the kind of person my mother is.

I knew it wasn't over. I knew I'd have to deal with it. That day came finally. Too soon.

It was just him that day. He walked up to me on the playground. I was still scared, but only of doing what I knew I'd have to do. I knew what he was going to say. I could see it in his eyes. And I was almost glad, because I knew that now we could get it over with, go on and do whatever had to be done.

"Hey," he said. "Where's your daddy?"

My head got to feeling light. Dizzy.

Your daddy's in the pen. He's a convick. My daddy told me about your daddy. He murdered somebody. He's a murderer.

I had the knife that was all I had of my daddy. A Case, the blades worn thin from twenty years of sharpening.

Killed somebody. Shot him down like a dog. And they ain't never gonna let him out of the pen.

More like an ice pick, really.

Cause he's in for life. Cause he's a murderer. And you ain't never gonna get to see your daddy again long as you live.

Thin, sharp. Cut your ass off. That he'd left on the washstand beside the cracked white pitcher and the white enamel bowl that held the dirty water she would take up and throw out into the back yard. Where the chickens we had kept the yard pecked bare. And the thin flowers tried to grow in the shade where she nursed them.

Did he say anything about your daddy? Don't you never. I don't care what you have to do. Let nobody talk about him.

It had turquoise handles, and the steel was rusted brown except where it was shiny on the razor edge from the last time he'd sharpened it. I took it. It was mine. He never gave it to me, and she never gave it to me, but it was mine.

Your daddy's a lowdown murderin' son of a bitch. That's what my daddy said. You know what else my daddy said?

Everybody in London Hill was real surprised when I stabbed Matt Monroe one inch to the left of his heart. Everybody, I think, except my mother. I know Matt Monroe could hardly believe it.

We were down at one end of the ward by ourselves. There wasn't anybody else in the place but a few other guys like this guy Braiden. Guys who'd never go home. Guys who'd given all they had and then some. Leftover guys.

After a while, my head cleared, and I could raise up. I sat up in the bed and looked at him.

"You want a beer?" he said.

I guess I looked at him a little funny.

"Brewskie," he said. "I got some Bud under my bed, man. Get you one if you want it."

I looked at his bed. A long white sheet hung down the

side of it, long enough to hide anything that might be under there. There wasn't any need in asking him if he was serious. I could tell that he was.

"Get you one if you want one," he said.

I looked around. There wasn't a nurse anywhere around.

"Reach under this bed here. My little cooler under there. Go on," he said.

I swung my legs over the side of the bed slowly. I put my feet on the floor. The tiles were cool. My head still felt a little woozy, but I rocked back and forth to make sure I wouldn't fall when I stood up. I eased off the bed gradually, and didn't fall. He was pawing at the sheet with one of his nubs. And there it was, a little red-and-white Igloo cooler sitting just inside the frame. I got down on one knee and opened it, and there were four bottles of Bud in some ice that was almost melted. I got one and got back in bed with it and put it under the covers. In a little bit I opened it. And in another little bit I took a drink of it. Somebody had left my cigarettes and lighter on a little table beside the bed, so I got a Marlboro to go with it. Things didn't seem nearly as bad after I got that cigarette lit. I knew then that there were loopholes. I knew then that if you found the right loop, you could leap. I knew then that eventually I could get my ass out of there, and home. It gave me a little hope.

I looked at Braiden. He was smiling a little.

"Thanks, man. That makes me feel about two hundred percent better."

"Sure, man. Man got to have something in here."

I leaned back on the pillow. The beer was between my legs and it was cold on my equipment down there. It didn't matter. I hadn't been using it anyway. Not until I met Beth. And I didn't really know if I'd gotten to use it then or not. I couldn't remember a thing about what happened after it started raining. All I remembered was before. I remembered that plenty.

I looked around at some of the other guys on the far end of the ward. Some were moaning. Some were tranked out. A few in wheelchairs were talking quietly to each other, smoking cigarettes. Twenty-two years. I knew I had to talk to him, hell, I was drinking his beer. He was probably desperate for some conversation. He wasn't having any fun life. There was no telling how long it had been since somebody had come in and talked to him.

I looked at him and thought: How would it be to be flat on your back with no arms or legs, unable to blow your nose, turn on a TV, smoke a cigarette, drink a beer, read a book, wipe your ass?

"Do you wish you were dead?" I said. I held the beer under the covers and looked straight into his eyes. They burned.

"Not a minute don't go by," he said.

I was afraid of that.

Could tell he didn't want to talk. It was something bothering him. He kept looking around at everybody but me. Probably didn't want to look at me. Couldn't much blame him. So I closed my eyes. Went somewhere.

Ookamalawandamanda. Your crocodiles on my side of the river. You get your crocodiles back on your side of the river. I got some warriors down here, whip your ass if I tell em to. Now this a big king from across the river, big fat belly like a pregnant woman. Old big navel hole sticking out. Don't look like no royalty. Got some leopard skin jockey shorts. And he gonna come over here and tell me like he the game warden. All he wanting is just to rape and pillage my village anyhow. Run off all my elephants. Drink all my rice beer. Might could run this fool off with a show of force. He probably got fifteen or twenty dusky young maidenhead maidens.

Listen, fool. I ain't got them crocs on no leash.

Listen, chump. You got about twenty-four seconds to get them crocs hemmed up and swarmed up over here on your bank. Cause they over here raping my crocs.

Aw yeah?

Yeah.

Say who?

Say me. How many men you got in your village done killed a lion with a blowgun?

Man we don't mess with no blowguns. We lasso em and whip em with sticks and make em tote water for us. And y'all over there gettin your asses eat up by em.

Aw man you tellin it now. Man you think I's born yesterday. Man we killed us a elephant yesterday.

One bout three days old?

Say what, man this thing was grown! What you mean talking this kinda shit to me?

Well man you over here talking it to me. Come over here gonna get on my ass over some reptiles I ain't even got no control over. When all the time what we been needing to do is get us up a village *alliance* like with some nets and stuff to make it safe for our women to go down to the river and wash clothes and stuff. Man I done lost three wives to them damn crocodiles. Pretty wives. Man, don't be over here talking no shit to me if you ain't had a wife eat up yet. Cause I done had three eat up.

Aw man.

Well. That what I'm telling you. You over here talking shit, you don't even know what going on.

I didn't know you had three wives eat up, man.

Cause you don't never come over here and see me. Unless you want to raise hell about something.

Well you know I'm busy, man. I mean, you know how it is. You a king too.

You could come over here and see me once in a while. Have a rice beer or two with me. It ain't like you no damn three hundred miles away or nothing.

I know it, man.

And then come over here wanting to get on my ass. Them damn lions *run* when they see my boys coming through. Cause they done seen they mamas and they daddies get run through with our spears. And you over here wanting to mess with us. Shit. Man we would strictly nilate y'all. Just nilate y'all.

He said, "Hey, man," and I opened my eyes for just a second.

Well I'm sorry about the misunderstanding over the crocs, man. It won't happen no more.

Aw it's cool, man. Don't even mention it. Listen here, why don't y'all come on over tonight, man? We'll have us a feast. We'll kill some of them damn crocodiles and have us some crocodile-tail soup.

Well. We might. You got anything to drink?

Shit. Has we got something to drink? Man we got two hundred and forty-two bushels of rice beer over here. You got any young nubiles over there?

Aw we got the nubiles, man. We got nubiles running around all over the place. We got more nubiles than we got anything. We short on warriors and rice beer is what we short on.

Well y'all come on over about dark, then. We'll build us up a big fire and do some dancing around it and all. My son gonna kill him his first lion in a few days and we gonna have a few manhood rites for him.

Y'all got some big fat ones over here?

Aw yeah, man, we got some nice big fat ones over here. They done laid around over here eating my cows up and done got fat and lazy. We done let em get so fat they can't hardly walk and we gonna hunt em before long. Thin a few of em out. You know lion hunting ain't what it used to be.

You can say that again.

Shoot. My daddy used to use me for bait. Oo and when them summitches was coming after you you could hear their stomachs growling. Them summitches'd hunt you. These boys now don't know how rough we had it when we was coming up.

"Hey, man," he said. "You awake?"

Aw naw. These younguns now don't know what it's like. Man the world going to shit, ain't it?

I tell you. It is. Well come on over about dark, then, man.

What you want us to bring?

Shit. Just bring yourself. We got everything over here we need. You might bring a few of them nubiles if you got a few extra.

We got em. How many you want?

I don't care. Hell, ten or fifteen, twenty, thirty. However many you want to bring.

I can bring however many you want.

Bring fifty.

"You got another one of these beers I can have?" he said.

I opened my eyes and looked at him. "Don't never stay here," I said. "Got too many places to go."

The white man always look so puzzled. Don't look like he know what to say. Met some good ones, though. Some motherfuckers, too. Man can say that about any race.

He thought I was crazy, probably. But I meant in here was like prison. Ain't no bars on the windows, but ain't many ways to leave.

I told him to go on and get him another beer. Told him to get all of them if he wanted them. Told him we'd have some more coming later.

He got out of bed and looked around and got him another one. Got back in the bed with it, lit him a cigarette. Man he had a messed-up face. I was looking at him and thinking about it and wondering what had happened to him. That's when he started talking to me. And he like to never stopped.

"I was in a rifle company. Joined the marines when I was eighteen. I had to go. The army was fixing to draft me. Back when they had that lottery system, my birthday was number one. And hell, I'd already had my physical, I was 1-A. So I knew I was gone. The lady who ran the draft board in town called my mama and told her I had about two weeks to join something if I wanted to, because after that the army would get me. So I joined the marines. I figured they were the toughest thing going. My old man, he . . . he really resisted me going. Both of them did. It was getting worse and worse all the time. I guess you were over there before I was. He was in World War II.

He stayed in it for four years. Walked all the way across Europe with the infantry, was wounded once. He knew what it was like to have to fight with a rifle. He taught me how to shoot. We'd hunt squirrels with a .22. Shoot em in the head.

"He was in prison for a while. A long time ago. Twice.

"I was over there within six months. Did it smell like something dead the whole time you were over there? Same here. I thought I'd never get out of there alive. I couldn't sleep for a long time. I couldn't sleep at all without a rifle next to me. I was usually always the biggest so I usually always kept the M60. Twenty-six pounds. I loved that damned gun. Kept it clean. I could by God shoot it, too."

We went hunting for the last time together about a week before I left. Mama said he wouldn't even go after I left. Wouldn't even take his gun out of the rack and clean it. Didn't care anything about it if I wasn't with him, she said.

We parked on the Hartsfield Hill and went off down the bluff to hunt toward the bottom. He taught me how to get down in a dry creekbed and just slip up through there. He went off to the left and gave me the best place. He always did that. He'd always give me something before he'd take it for himself. It was hard to get used to having him again after not having him for so long. Or just be able to visit him on the weekends. He said the law always worked better for the rich than it did for the poor. I guess he was right.

I guess we hunted for about an hour and a half. We had

a big sweet gum tree we always met at right before dark. I think I had five by the time I got up there. I'd been hearing him shoot once in a while, but he only had two. He wasn't thinking about squirrels.

He was stretched out on the ground smoking a cigarette under the tree when I got there. I unloaded my rifle and sat down beside him. He had a little whiskey on him. He was sipping on it. I could tell he had something on his mind. Something he wanted to tell me. He never would talk very loud in the woods. And he didn't ever talk much anyway. He was one of those people. The ones you don't want to fuck with.

Finally he looked at me and said I didn't have any idea what I was getting into. He said two or three hundred Americans were dying every week, and none of them thought it would be him. He said in war you've got to kill all the people you can to try and keep yourself alive. The less of them, he said, the better the chances for you. He said to keep my eyes open, look and listen and learn all I could. Trust nobody. Depend on nobody.

He said what he'd done was something he'd had to do. He said he'd known what it would cost before he did it, but he went on and did it anyway because it was what he had to do, that he didn't have any choice. He said now that he finally had us back, he was losing me. And he'd thought about me every day. He said all he wanted me to do was take care of myself. Listen to what they taught me. Because he wanted me to come back home to him. And not in some goddamn coffin.

Man can go crazy laying around a place like this. That's the truth. Take me early this morning when he first got here. Sun come up like it always do. Yeah, sun also rise for Braiden Chaney. Me in my bed. Window frame start getting lighter, the floor, sheets on my bed. The morning always the quietest time in this place. Nobody stirring. Everybody sleeping. Television's off. Which I don't watch them fools no way. Nurses are all drinking coffee, getting ready to go home. Diva too. In the mornings I always know it will be a long time before I'll see her again. Know I can't wait that long for her. Why I have to go somewhere. Go somewhere yesterday, go somewhere today, another place tomorrow. Can't stay here.

But people out there in that city coming to life. Waking up, cooking breakfast, hating to get out of the bed. They'd been in one long enough, they wouldn't. But hold on. Wasn't bitter. Just tired. Lots of them getting their kids ready for school. They drive by here, they ain't thinking about who's in here. They watching for the red lights. I hear them come by. I hear their horns. I know what they do. They go to their jobs and do things with their hands, legs carry them from one place to another.

World's too big. People don't know what other people doing. Ain't no way to keep up with everything that's happening. Too much stuff, and too many people. Only thing you can know of the world's your little bitty piece of it.

I guess the Lord knows it all. He made it. But I never could see how He kept up with it.

I am wishing they'd hurry up with my breakfast. Want to go on and get that out of the way. I'm wondering how much he gonna talk to me anyway. I got lions to kill, and tribes to fight off. Got maidens. Many of them. Many beautiful ones I can touch with my hands.

"I was wounded three times before this happened. I was shot twice one day and then another day I got hit with some shrapnel. Nothing major. I think I got three weeks sick leave altogether for that. Went to the Philippines for R and R one time. I started to not even go back. If I'd had any sense I wouldn't've. But I was just a kid, I didn't know any better. The whole world was out there, Europe, Canada, Mexico, Australia. I went back. I was back in country four days when I got hit.

"Damn that beer's good and cold. I wish somebody'd come in here and tell me something. I don't even know what the hell happened. I guess I had another one of my fits. Spells. That's why I'm here, I know. They're scared to operate on me. My speech might be affected. Something about my brain, and scar tissue. They did plastic surgery on me and I went through all that. They'd do some more if I'd let them. I just said fuck it. I can live without it. Nobody has to look at me if they don't want to.

"It was one morning we hadn't even been out. It had been raining all night, was still raining. Monsoons had set in. They called for us to fall out. We'd all been drinking beer. That's where I started drinking. I'd never even had a beer when I went in. We were all about half drunk that morning. An army patrol had been hit about two miles west of us. I think they'd killed five or six of ours. They'd done medevaced everybody out and called artillery in on it, but they wanted us to go check it out. Get a body count if there was one. We had this little chickenshit second lieutenant just out of Quantico they'd give us, he was raring to go.

"He just had got there. He was running around, raising hell, cussing, trying to get us ready to go. Took us about an hour to get over there. Mud everywhere you walked. And I was toting that machine gun. I was tired and ready to sit down. Finally we got over there. They'd done blowed everything all to shit. This one little area we were in, there was just a couple of little trees left standing. That was it. They had some leaves up in the top of them but we didn't think anything about it. Hell, they'd blowed craters in the ground big as swimming pools. And we found a couple of people. Found two or three, parts of a couple more. You couldn't tell how many. The lieutenant was trying to get everybody to pile it all together so he could get a body count. Crazy sumbitch. I don't know why they didn't shoot his ass.

"Hell, maybe it was because I was the machinegunner. Maybe they wanted to kill the firepower first. That's a good tactic. I was sitting down smoking a cigarette on the bank of this little creek. I guess it was a rocket grenade but I never did find out for sure. It hit about twenty, thirty feet in front of me. I think I had my head down, taking a drag. I guess that saved me from being killed, catching a piece in the throat or something. But I always wore a flak jacket. It seemed like it went off in my face. And I knew I was hurt pretty bad. But I got up. Had blood all over me. Running off my chin, handfuls of it. I felt of my face. It was all tore up. I could touch some bone. I started walking over to this boy I knew and it was like somebody hit me with his fist in the top of the head. Sniper. That was it. I remember it happening. I just don't remember anything after it. Not until I woke up in the hospital. That was four weeks later. In the Philippines. Subic Bay. They discharged me after that. Medical. One guy said they couldn't operate, that the bullet went in too deep. Another one said he might could get it out, that it's in three pieces. But he said it might leave me mute. Unable to talk. It's scar tissue in there too. Causes these seizures. So every once in a while, I just pass out. I might go six months without it happening. It has hit me twice in one day. Sometimes there's a warning to it and sometimes it ain't. Sometimes it just happens.

"I don't know what happened this time. I was with a girl. A young lady. I'd just met her a day or two before. We were in a car.

"She's like me, she's not . . . normal. But she was good to me. She could stand me. But I don't know what happened. I don't know where she is now. I don't know where anybody is. I've got to get out of here."

He was talking, I didn't want to interrupt him. I told him I had somebody to take care of me. Didn't want to tell him who it was yet. Thought I'd just let him see her. Cause she's fine. Finest thing in this place.

Naw but I was thinking about what it must have been like for him, face full of shrapnel one second and a bullet in the head the next. And coming home to a mama whose boy ain't got his own face no more. Not knowing when he was gonna fall. Said while ago I'd seen every kind of man and injury there was come in here.

Hadn't seen nobody like him.

I didn't care for him talking about what happened to

him. Some of em you can't get nothing out of em. Just clam up, go off. Be mental cases. Some of em can take it and some can't. Plenty of them that ain't nothing physical wrong with them. Their minds is just gone. Have to push them around in a wheelchair, guys in their thirties and forties, like old crippled people. They crippled, all right. Just in a different way.

It do something to you to kill another person. It ain't no dog lying there. Somebody. A person, talk like you, eat like you, got a mind like you. Got a soul like you. And everybody have to handle that in a different way. Cause that a heavy thing to handle. That something you don't forget. You pull the trigger on somebody, it pulled forever. Ain't like dropping a bomb on him, where you way up high in the air and can't see what's happening on the ground, even though you know it's bad.

You look in somebody's eyes, then kill him, you remember them eyes. You remember that you was the last thing he seen.

"Usually I just stay in my room. I live with my mother and my brother. But I don't see them much. They get the red-ass if they have to look at me too much.

"Ah shit. I ought not say that. Hell. I know it hurts them to look at me. I just try to spare them. Stay out of the way. I've got plenty of stuff to do in my room anyway. I keep my headphones on most of the time. I've got a bunch of books and movies.

"He's my little brother. He's almost as big as I am. Only brother I've got. I hope they're here with me. I hope somebody's here with me."

* * *

He didn't even remember Daddy. But it wasn't any wonder. Daddy'd been gone so long and he'd never seen him to begin with. I'm sure he felt funny. Having to hug this man he knew was his daddy but he never had seen him. Just seen pictures and stuff. Stuff he brought home from the war. Medals, and patches off his uniform. He sent home a luger in the pocket of an overcoat but they x-rayed the package and saw the luger and took it out and sent the coat on home. He was in Berlin at the end.

He didn't want us to meet him in town when he came home from the pen the first time. He didn't want our reunion to be held in a bus station. He caught the bus but when he got to town he got a taxi to bring him home. I think Mama was glad of that. But Max didn't know what to do. Didn't know how to act. Daddy kept wanting him to sit in his lap, and he kept going, but after a while he'd get down. He wouldn't hardly open his mouth. Finally what he did was sit down on the floor and put his arm around Daddy's ankle. Just sat there holding his ankle.

I guess Max was five or six when he came home. I was eleven or twelve.

He was drunk when he killed that guy. I wish he hadn't done it. Maybe things would have been different. Or better.

I guess he was drunk on every major fuckup he made. Except for the last one. And it wasn't even his fault.

Talk a minute then he'd hush a minute. Talk a minute then hush a minute. Like he wasn't here but half the time. I started to ask him one time if he knowed his face was all scratched up. What I figured, he'd done been in a car wreck. Was how come they had him in here, probably, too, was probably treating him for the car wreck.

But it look like they wouldn't let him be driving if he was gonna pass out. Don't look like they'd even let him have a license. I wouldn't want to be meeting somebody coming down the road passed out. Might run over you.

Was about to get the hunger on me. They come in then down at the far end of the ward. I asked him was he gonna eat anything but he just shook his head. He was steady sucking that beer. Finished that one and put it under his pillow. Which I ain't got nothing against a man drinking in the morning if he want to.

Have to lay here every morning and watch them give everybody else their breakfast before they give me mine. Don't take long, though. Ain't many left. So many done passed away. Only new ones we had in a while was from Beirut. Had one from Grenada but he went home, too. Home to his Lord.

Talked to him some. Little old private. Course they give him some medals one time and made him a meritorious promotion to lance corporal. Jumped him two grades all at once. He was machinegunned too. Only he was shot all through the body. Kept having leaks inside of him. They'd sew up one and it would last a while and then another one would bust and they'd rush him down to surgery and sew it up. He hovered between life and death for three weeks before they brought him up here. He said his insides was about like a old bicycle innertube. Shit blood all the time. They kept him high was the only way he could stand it. Would come over here and pull his wheelchair up beside my bed and do card tricks. And would juggle, too. He come over here one night and we got to drinking beer and he got about half drunk and started juggling three Budweiser bottles and kept them going a while. He was from Port Angeles, Washington, and he would have been twenty if he'd lived one more day. Lance Corporal John Davis Williams, USMC. Semper fi, bro.

They come on down with my breakfast. Every morning I have me three over easy with two sausage patties and two strips of bacon and one piece of country ham, and two orders of homefries with just a little ketchup and two glasses of milk and one OJ. Don't let em try to give me no coffee. Done been burnt too many times. Could probably let it cool off and sip it with a straw. But they ain't got time for that shit.

I waited until they fed me and then I told him to go on and tell me what he was fixing to tell me cause it wasn't gonna be long before they come in here to mop the floor and stuff and change sheets.

I told him I knew he was scared and everything and it was a strange place for him to wake up in but everything would be all right and would be even more all right when dark come. I told him to talk to me. I told him I knew where he was coming from.

"Well, hell. I might as well. Her name's Beth. It was raining, I know that. It just had started. I'll just tell you what happened from the start. My daddy died about six months ago. I think I told you we used to farm. I started picking cotton when I was six years old. Back in the old days. You remember them old days? Back when they paid two cents a pound? Hell, you know how it was, you're from down there in the Delta. It's flat, ain't it? We're up in the hills. It's a lot different, I guess. The ground ain't as good. We haven't got two hundred million years of dinosaur shit up there.

"I don't usually talk this much. I usually don't have

anybody to talk to. I've got a lot of books. I'm a big reader. Plus I like movies. That's about all I do, read and watch movies. When I'm not passed out.

"He was pretty bad to drink. Hell, I'm pretty bad to drink myself. That's probably why I'm in here, drinking too much. I have these seizures more often if I'm drinking. I can't hardly get through it straight, though."

I thought for a while they might send me down to prison and I remembered wondering if they'd let me stay in the same cell with him. I mean for stabbing Matt Monroe. I kept wondering if they'd have a uniform with stripes in my size.

Finally they didn't do anything to me. Matt didn't come close to dying or anything. By about an inch. I guess if I'd killed him they'd have had to do something with me, but I don't know what. I guess they could have waited until I got grown and then sent me off.

But even with the way things happened, I imagine my mama would have shot the first son of a bitch who stepped in our yard to get me.

"Hell, they've been talking about maybe doing an operation on me for a long time. I don't know how many times I've passed out. A bunch. At one time I kept up with it. I had a logbook. How long I stayed awake, what time I passed out, what time I woke up. What were the circumstances when I passed out. But it got to be too much trouble. I started seeing how much time I was losing. All that did was just depress me. I was depressed enough already. So I just quit doing it.

"It's best to just not think about it. I mean it doesn't do any good. Hell, I'm happy enough. Nobody messes with me. Of course some people are scared of me. Little kids especially. I guess I hate that worse than anything. I don't get out much in the daytime. Usually just at night. I don't see my mother and my brother too much. I don't hide from them. I'm not hiding from them. I'm just staying in my room."

She's on a big death kick. Has been ever since Daddy died. Wants to join him. She lays in her room every night and prays to die. She thinks if she prays hard enough, God'll let her die. Or make her die. You can't talk any sense to her. So finally I just quit. I just started staying in my room all the time. Max can't do anything with her. And when he gets off from work he doesn't want to listen to that shit. You can't blame him. It's a wonder he hasn't moved out. Both of us are probably stopping him from finding him a woman to marry and moving out and starting a family of his own.

Asking God to take her. How does anybody even know what God is? Other than love. I told her one time to look at it like this: Say you live off in the woods somewhere, like this tribe they found a while back. And you live a pretty good life, don't murder or rape anybody, and then die. And you've never had a chance to receive the word of God just because the missionaries never could find you.

Do you think God is going to send you to hell just because you were never allowed the opportunity to read a Bible? I said Hell, what if you couldn't even read? She didn't know how to answer that.

"Daddy started drinking a lot worse after I came back in the shape I'm in. We lost our place. He'd got us to where we had over two hundred acres. Now we've got two. He got deeper and deeper in debt. They finally foreclosed on him. It's just a bunch of shit."

He closed up on me again. Just turned his head away. Just get to going good and he'd hush. Eyes would roll away from me and you could tell he was thinking about something else.

It didn't matter. Maybe he just didn't want to talk while they was mopping the floor and all. We didn't talk then. Aw I spoke to Hazel and them while they was cleaning up and changing bed sheets and all but he wouldn't let them change his. Said he hadn't been on them long enough to need changing.

I didn't know what was the matter with him. But finally they left and he started talking again. After he got him another beer he did.

"I don't know how many nights ago this was now. I don't know how long I've been out. But I was in there in my room trying to read. The power was off and it was so hot you couldn't stand to stay in there. Couldn't even run the fan without the generator, and I was out of gas.

"I've got one of these little Honda generators. The power goes off so much, I bought one. I ran me a pipe through the wall to take the exhaust outside. I got tired of watching a movie and having the power go off. It's pretty neat. You can hook your TV and your VCR into one outlet and the little sumbitch'll just sit there and hum. Tell TVA to get fucked.

"Well, she was in there in her room, moaning and all. Praying to die. And Max came in. He goes into her room every night to check on her. And I mean she was just screaming and moaning and praying God to die until I got tired of listening to it. So I just climbed out the window and went down the road to the beer store. I usually just climb out the window instead of walking through the house. If I walk through the house and they see me, they try to talk me into coming out of my room. So it's easier to just climb out the window. No muss, no fuss. That way they don't know if I'm busy being passed out in there or what.

"I took a couple of beers with me, hell, it's about three miles to the beer store. And it was hot as a fresh-fucked fox in a forest fire. I was about out of beer and ice both. Aw hell they told me in the Philippines that they could operate on my head, but it was a chance they might damage me. I didn't want to take the chance. I'm on hundred percent disability anyway. That's what I live off of. I just put up with these spells when I have them and wake up later. I wish to hell I knew what happened this time.

"I went around behind the house and looked in her window. I couldn't tell if she was asleep or not. It was dark in there. I've tried to take care of her. Hell, I know it hurts her to not see me, but it hurts her to see me, too. So I just stay in my room a lot. I've got plenty to do.

"Night's about the only time I go out. It's better for me to move around then. I walk on the side of the road so if I pass out some son of a bitch won't come along and run over me in the middle of the road thinking I'm a goddamn dog or something.

"It's kind of nice not to have to work. It's nice to have that check coming in every month. I keep myself entertained. That's about all I do. I guess I was wasting my life until I met her. She'll probably be here later on. Probably just any time. She hasn't met my family yet. She'll come see about me when she finds out where I am. I'll introduce you to her when she gets up here. She's got a car. She can carry me home.

"What it was, she was working in this store I always go to. And it was like close to midnight when I left the house. I took this shortcut down through this old dry creek, Moore Creek. That's where we were parked when I had this fit, I reckon. Or whatever I had. That's the last thing I remember. We pulled down in there so nobody would see us. People go down there and fuck all the time. It's a perfect place. The road's not open anymore. The bridge caved in and they never built it back when they built the new road. They just took that curve out of it."

I remember when it was all gravel. We walked everywhere we went. And later on carrying Max. That was while Daddy was still gone. A few days we hired out to Doyle Edwards to chop cotton and make a little money. Four dollars a day. He didn't want to pay me four because he said I was too little. And she told him to go up to our place and look and see if there was any grass in our cotton. Bad the way a man, some men, anyway, will try to take advantage of a woman when her man's not around. Couldn't leave Max with anybody. There wasn't anybody to leave him with. Had to leave him on a blanket in the shade by the creek at the end of the rows.

All day long in that sun. Swinging a hoe. For four dollars. To get something to eat. God.

He was talking and I was just looking at him. I kept looking at them scratches on his face. Wondered who put them there. And if he even knowed they was there.

He kept talking about this girl, this girl, and I thought, Man, where you gonna find a woman that would mess with you? Cause I mean his face was messed up big time. Just scar tissue. Places he had hair and places wasn't no hair. Skin grafts. Aw he had a piece of a face but it wasn't a real face. Them guys I guess do the best they can with what they got to work with. And he'd done said himself they'd do some more if he'd let them. I guess he'd done been in and out of VA hospitals so much he didn't want to see another one.

I guess that was why he never did ask where he was. I guess he figured it didn't make no difference.

"So anyhow I walked on over to the store and drank a beer on the way. I knew it was getting late. They're not supposed to sell beer after midnight. But I went to high school with this old boy who owns it. He always lets me have it. Well I got over there and he wasn't there. And it was almost one o'clock. I saw this girl sitting behind the counter, and hell, I didn't know her. And you know, somebody who looks like me, coming in on her at that hour of the night. Shit, I didn't know what to do. I didn't figure she'd let me have it. But I wanted some beer. I was gonna go back home and smoke some dope and watch *One Flew Over The Cuckoo's Nest*. Watch old Will smother Jack again. Loved him so damn much he killed him. Which would be a hell of a thing to have to do for somebody. And then when he tears that damn sink out of the floor and throws it through the window. I'll get high and rewind that last three or four minutes four or five times.

"So I didn't know what to do. I was just standing out on the front there. She was watching me. I guess she thought I was some kind of a creep. I guess I looked like I was.

"But I went on in and spoke to her, you know, and she spoke, asked me what I wanted. I told her I wanted some beer. She said it was after midnight and she couldn't sell me any.

"She's got blond hair. She's built real nice. I was looking at her breasts and I know she saw it. She's really just a kid. But very grown up somehow. I've sort of got some guilty feelings about some of this. But I noticed she was dressed kind of funny for as hot as it was. She had on long pants and a long-sleeved shirt. I mean it was air-conditioned in the store, but it wasn't *that* air-conditioned. I didn't mean to stare at her. She just looked so good it was hard not to.

"I told her I knew Earl and all and we went to high school together and he always let me have it if it was late. And she says Earl was the one who told her not to sell it after midnight and Earl was the one who told her he'd fire her if he caught her doing it. So I felt like a dumbass. But I got kind of pissed off. I mean, you go over there and get a hole shot in your head and then come home and have to listen to some shit from a teenager about buying a little beer after hours. Hell. She wasn't going to sell it to me. So I just politely went down to the cooler and got two six-packs of Bud and carried it and put it on the counter.

"She asked me what the hell I thought I was doing. I told her I was buying some beer. I told her my name was Walter and I lived down the road and I came in there and got it all the time. I told her not to get upset. She said she wasn't upset, she just didn't want to lose her job. I told her there wasn't any reason to be scared of me. But, hell, it was late, and she was alone in there. She was upset. But I knew what the beer cost. I already had the money out. The sales tax, too. She told me I'd better just get out of there before she called the law. I wasn't worried about that. I knew I could get away before the law got there. Unless I passed out first.

"Well, I put my money up on the counter. She wasn't going to ring it up at first. I said fine, don't ring it up. But I said there the money was anyway. And she just changed all of a sudden. I remember what she said. She said I'm sorry for looking at you. For staring at you, she said. I said well hell, that was okay, most people did. And she reached under the counter and got me a sack. Rang it up. Sacked up my beer. I told her I didn't mean to scare her. But I told her, a lot of people were scared of me. She said she wasn't scared, it was just the first job she'd ever had.

"Hell, I didn't know what to say. I wasn't thinking about trying to get over on her or anything. I figured I'd just take my beer and go back home and watch Nicholson. Get high. She asked me if I was walking and I said yeah. Then she asked me how far away I lived. I told her it was about three miles. She said she knew me, that she'd heard of me, that she'd heard Earl mention me before. And hell, we just got to talking. She said I just surprised her because I walked up and she didn't hear me, just looked out the window and I was standing there. She asked me if I was fixing to walk back home. I said yeah, but I was thinking about opening me one of those beers before I started, though. If she didn't care. She said naw, she didn't care. So I got me one. Then I asked her if she wanted one. She said she wasn't supposed to drink on duty. I told her she wasn't supposed to sell me the shit, either. I tried to give her one twice. She wouldn't take one, though. Went back there and got her a Miller out of the cooler. I thought about getting me some chicken, but hell, they'd cooked it about dinnertime you could tell. It had flies on it and all. I decided I didn't want any chicken.

"So hell she came on back up there and sat down and opened her beer and lit her a cigarette and told me her name was Beth. I mean it was getting cozy all of a sudden and I couldn't understand why. And then guess what she does? Starts asking me about going over there. Hell. You don't want to talk about that shit unless it's with somebody who was over there. I didn't want to talk about it. Told her I didn't want to.

"So she asked me if I knew why I scared her so bad. She reached under the counter and pulled out a dinner plate loaded with sensimilla, about a lid. She'd been cleaning it. Asked me if I wanted to get high. I said *Hell* yeah. So she rolled one up right quick. It was as tight as a Marlboro. And I mean rolled it in like nothing flat. She said we just needed to go outside and smoke it. So I followed her out back there and we lit it up. We sat on this old drink cooler out there. I knew it was bad shit when I first hit it. I got fucked up almost immediately. It was the best I'd had in a while and I just kept smoking it. I think that's what messed me up. I've noticed that it happens more often when I've been smoking a lot. So I try not to do it all the time. We smoked the whole thing, though. I couldn't hardly talk. I got to looking at her again. And she didn't care, man. She was sweet.

"We finally went on back inside. Got our beers. I gave her some Visine for the redeye. I was ready for the movie then. I knew it would take me all night to walk back home, just from everything slowing down. I got to thinking about how heavy those two six-packs of beer were gonna get. But, hell, I had to go. So I told her I was fixing to. She asked me what I's gonna do. I told her just go home and watch a movie. And I don't even know what in the hell we said. But the next thing I knew she'd done locked the store up and we were out in her car. I remember taking a drink or two of beer. And then the next thing I knew I was waking up."

He hushed for a while. Turned his head away. I closed my eyes. I wanted to have a dream about Jesus and I had it. Had part of it and made up part of it. I've seen Jesus. He just looks like you and me. You could meet Him out on the street and you wouldn't know Him. I know why He ain't come back. The world would probably find some way to kill Him again. Don't think He don't know how the world is. Seen that when He come down the first time. He give this thing His okay, in a way. He sat on the side of my bed. Had gold dust on His sandals. Sat there scraping it off with one of them little wooden sticks they look down your throat with.

He said, "Listen, Braiden. Ain't nothing for you to do but lay here. I can't take your life. This guy over here, that's something else. I ain't got no control over what you talk him into. But be careful. You treading on shaky ground here. You know what I'm talking about."

I said, "Jesus, you know I'm suffering."

"Yeah, I know it. A lot of people are suffering. I know you believe in Me and God and all. I know you been laying here a long time. Lot of people been laying in a lot of places a long time. A lot of them longer than you."

I said, "Jesus, I know everything You saying. You know my mama, don't You?"

He wouldn't look at me. "Yeah, I know your mama. I ain't met many better than her. Don't bring your mama into this. She's happy where she's at. But don't ask no more questions along that line. Some things you ain't meant to know."

"Well I figgered You knowed her. She the one raised me. But listen here, how long You reckon I gonna have to lay here if nothin don't happen?"

The Lord looked a little uneasy then. And see, He can't tell no lie. I mean, He whipped the coondog shit out of them moneychangers in His temple, but that was something else. He *ain't* gonna lie.

He said, "I wish you wouldn't ask me that, Braiden." Then He looked around. "You ain't got any cigarettes in here, have you?"

I told Him they was some over here in this drawer. I told Him I didn't know what He wanted to be smoking for.

He got up and went over to the table and got a couple out. Said I just didn't know what all He had to put up with. Asked me did I want Him to light me one while He was lighting Him one. I said yessir and please.

He got His going and got me one going and then sat there holding it for me while I smoked. You could tell He had a lot on His mind. And here I was worrying Him some more.

"Look, Braiden. I been around a long time. You know God made man in His image. Made him out of dust and blowed the breath of life into him. Give him Eden, and give him Eve. And they had two sons. And look what happened there. It ain't been any different ever since. There has always been wars, and there is always going to be wars. Always been people mean enough to kill babies. Always going to be. Some people kill people all their lives, and then get caught, and sentenced to death, and then they want to be Christians. Just to keep from getting fried. And We can't keep them out. You wouldn't believe how many death-row murderers We've got up there right now."

"That what You stand for, though," I said. He let me take a drag and then pulled it away. Thumped some ashes in the ashtray.

"Yeah, well, but I mean they've done stuff that just makes you sick to hear about it. And some little girl or somebody had to go through it. And then she's got to run into him up there. It just makes for awkward conversation, Braiden."

I flat out asked Him: "How long I gonna have to lay here, Jesus?"

He looked sad when I said that. He picked up His cigarette and looked out the window. One of them helicopters was starting to come down on the pad. Jesus looked awful sad.

"One more for me," he said. I guess they was somebody dead on it.

"Jesus," I said.

"You better talk right to this guy."

"How long?"

"I can't promise anything."

"You know, though. Don't You, Lord?"

"Yeah. I know."

I ought not've done it. Raised my voice. Not to Him. "Then tell me! How long? How much longer I got to put up with this? Look how long I done put up with it!"

Sure oughten to have done it. Made Him hot. Seen why that little fig tree withered when it didn't have no figs and He cursed it. Woo. Like to withered me.

"You don't like living?" He said. "Life's what He gave you, all of us."

And damn if I didn't mess up again.

"He didn't intend for some of us to be fucked up like this."

Oo He looked at me like I was the serpent himself. Eyes went cold, and just for a second He forgot Who He was. Voice went down a notch or two.

"Don't you talk to me like that, Braiden. I don't like that word."

"All right, Lord," I said. "I'm sorry. I'm *sorry!* But patience is *hard* after twenty-two years! You blink Your eyes in that length of time! Not me! *Jesus,* Jesus!"

I got broke down then. He come over and patted me on the shoulder for a while. I got over it. I straightened myself up and He reached and got some Kleenex and wiped my nose and I got myself right.

Had my voice meek because I remembered what They said about the lambs.

"I just want to know if it gonna be much longer."

"No, Braiden. It won't be much longer."

"Thank you, Lord."

Then He was gone. I opened my eyes. My savior was looking at me. I think he was wanting another beer.

"I didn't know where I was when I woke up. There wasn't a sound anywhere. Like in the jungle at night when it's so quiet you know something's fixing to happen. I was lying on the front seat of her car. I had a bunch of dents in my face from being pressed up against the seat. I think she must have tried to move me at first. I was just too heavy for her. I'd burned a hole in my shirt with a cigarette. Spilled beer all over myself.

"It was getting daylight. I sat up and looked around. I didn't see her at first. I got me a cigarette and lit it. Beer was all down in the floorboards. I figured she was gone.

Then I saw her sitting on a bank by the roadside. We were on a dirt road up in the woods. She had her knees drawn up and her head down on her arms. I don't know if she'd been crying or what. I hated to even try to explain.

"I got out. I had to tell her what it was. She raised her head when the interior light came on. But I went ahead and shut the door. I didn't know what to tell her. It was awful. The truth won't always set you free.

"I walked over there where she was. Said I was sorry. I said I should have told her that it might happen. She didn't say anything for a minute. Finally she said it was okay, she just hated to lose her job. I told her I'd talk to Earl and tell him that I'd talked her into it. She said she guessed she'd better get on back and face the music.

"It was getting good daylight. I saw some crows flying by. I watched them until they went out of sight. She said she thought I'd died or something at first. Said Boy when it hits you, it hits you, don't it? She wanted to know what it was. I just told her it was a war wound. She said she guessed I didn't want to talk about it. I said Right, I don't want to talk about it.

"She got up and dusted off her pants. Told me to get in and she'd take me home. Hell, I didn't want her to take me home. I told her I could walk. She wouldn't hear it, though. She said she didn't want me to have to tote all that beer all the way home. I didn't really want to get back in with her. But I didn't want to tote that beer, either. So I got in.

"We didn't talk much. I opened me another beer. I don't know why it had to happen then. I couldn't believe it. I couldn't even believe I was in the car with her.

"We got out to the highway and I told her I could just get out there. She wouldn't hear that, either. Said she'd take me home. Hell, I didn't want to walk. Didn't want to do anything but go back to my room and hide. She took me on home. I guess Mother and Max saw me come in. She let me out right in front of the house. I got my beer out and I was trying to think of something to say. She said it was nice meeting me. And she did something really strange. Well, strange for me. She reached out and touched my hand. Said maybe we could talk sometime.

"So I said, hell, sure. But I didn't figure I'd see her again. She had to get on back and open the store. I was hoping Earl hadn't come by yet and didn't know the store had been closed half the night. I was hoping like hell he wouldn't fire her if he did. Because the whole thing was my fault. Anyway she left. And I went on in and went to bed."

It come to me then, see, that Walter was the one. Cause like Jesus was a vision, man. But He was here with me, in this room. Sat right here on my bed. Man.

See, Walter come in here and didn't know nothing. Didn't know they'd had him on the stretcher rolling him down the hall and he come alive and put one orderly's head through a fire extinguisher box, had to have fourteen stitches in his head, and broke another one's arm for him. Diva told me before she went home. I mean this morning before he even come in the ward. Said he was a wild man. Said his face was all clawed up from a accident down in Mississippi and she was just walking along behind the thing they was rolling him on. And said man this dude just raised up all of a sudden and grabbed this boy's head and slammed it like somebody dunking a basketball against that box on the wall. Took four of them to hold him, she said. And wouldn't have done it then if she hadn't got the needle in him right then. So I knowed. I knowed.

Hey, it's all right. I ain't manipulating nobody. Man just have to look at the whole thing himself.

He laid there a while thinking his own stuff. Had them eyes just staring out the window. And it ain't even nothing to see. Sky. Clouds.

He asked me if I was tired of him talking and I said Naw man, go on, I'm listening to you. So he started, about his mama and them, why they ain't with him, about his girl. He kept on talking about her, how she was gonna come and see him and all. But something was wrong. He acted like maybe he knowed more than he made out like he knowed. What he acted like was he knowed what had happened. I don't know. Ain't got to reading minds yet. But he had something heavy on his head, I tell you that.

He's talking about how she got her job at that store and he got his check every month. He's talking about getting married to this girl. Talking about buying a trailer. Then got to talking about movies. Got to talking about something called Doctor Strange *Glove*. And who all was in it and how he was gonna let her watch it and all of a sudden he jumped over on James Earl Jones. My *man*. Asked me did I know he was from Tallahatchie County, Mississippi, and I said Shit.

Said Man what you think I am a recluse? I mean I didn't raise up much. Raised up a little. I said Man I know of my people who is famous. I said What you think I do, just lay up here and be ignorant of everything?

I told him. We got a library here. Got plenty of good books, too. Only sometimes you might be wanting you a good book and don't know what you want. I mean you don't know the title or the arthur or none of that shit. All you got to do is just tell one of these striped ladies when they come around every afternoon you'd like something from the library and would she please get it. I told him one time I did that a long time ago, first time I did it, and well I said I want something about the Civil War. And this was a nice old lady. She went down there and brought me up about three or four big books on the Civil War with lots of pictures. And for a while she set there and turned the pages for me. Then she asked me would I like to see and read about the black soldiers in the Civil War and I looked at her and said Yes ma'am I believe I would. So we got to looking at that. Man them dudes looked bad back then. They some of em probably wasn't but one generation off the boat. And it told right there in the book that some of them was the most feared regiments in the war. Said man they'd go to the bayonets in a minute. And you ought to seen them things. About eighteen inches long, razor tips, run you through like a sword. And I thought, man, steal you from *one* country and take you to another and have to wind up fighting for *that* country. Makes sense, though. What they did to us. Take us from *our* country over to *their* country and make you fight for *that* country.

This old lady was good to me. She turned the pages for me a long time and then she got up and said she'd be back after a while. And which I got mad at her at first cause she'd stopped. Couldn't do nothing by myself. Look at the covers. Started thinking all kinds of bad shit about white people again. Cause I wanted to look at them books.

I told Walter after a while she come back. Had some stuff with her. It was two TV trays taped together on one end with this block of wood in the middle. Where one could lay flat on your lap and the other one stand up about forty-five degrees for you to lay a book on. So she laid that down on my nubs and it set there and she took one of them books and opened it up and it just laid there. I was fixing to thank her and I mean man I was feeling bad about what I'd been thinking about white people in general like how they was the ones got me in this mess to begin with when she said she'd done figured out how for me to turn the pages, too. I said Naw. She said Yeah. Pulled out two little old wood sticks, and some tape. Taped them damn sticks up here on my arms so I could reach down and just catch the corner of that page and turn it. Hold the other page down with the other stick. I mean it took a while to get good with it. But I could lay there and read any damn book I wanted to. Magazine. Newspaper.

And I told him that was how I knew all about James Earl Jones. Told him I read *Jet* a lot. I didn't tell him how long I stay on the page got the sister in the bikini in it. Or the trips I take on that.

But hell, I guess I fucked up anyway. Couldn't wait, see. Had to go on and just jump right on him with it. Too impatient.

Well he give me an opening anyway. Started talking about James Earl and *The Great White Hope*. And they just wasn't nothing he could tell me. Cause I did it, I know it, but I raised so much hell up here one night with these motherfuckers that I *made* em turn it over on WTBS at twelve-oh-five so I could watch it. I watched it, too. I mean, they can watch these game shows and shit operas all day long. I want to see me some *drama* when the sun go down. I don't want to be watching something thinking what's in the frigerator, I want to be watching something thinking What is this dude gonna do *now?*

But that's what we got on the movies about. I asked him had he seen a good one, a old one but a good one, about them young lions. He said yeah. Sort of settled back in the bed. Said it was a damn good movie. Went to naming the actors. Brando. Clift. Dean Martin. You could tell he liked that movie and had watched it more than once.

I asked him did he remember that German captain or whatever he was, the one who had that fine-looking snake that drank that vodka straight?

He said yeah, he remembered her. Said damn she was

fine. I said oom hoom she was. But I said You remember what happened to that guy? That German officer. Old Marlon's boss.

He said yeah, he got blinded and put in a hospital. He said but he was a dirty son of a bitch anyway. Said he shot that blinded guy after they ambushed his whole company. Said that's how the Germans was. Said he knew how the Germans was. Said didn't nobody have to tell him nothing about the Germans.

And I don't know why he went off on that. He didn't say nothing for a minute. I asked him did he remember what happened to that German officer in that movie. About old Marlon going to see him and him asking Marlon to bring him something. He looked like he was thinking about something a long way off. He nodded his head real slow. And everything slowed down when he looked at me. Said it was a bayonet, and I said, yeah, that was right.

I asked him did he remember when he saw that movie the first time sitting there thinking about what that guy wanted that bayonet for? And he said yes, he did.

I asked him what did he think about that.

All he did was look at me.

Then he whispered, where I could just *barely* hear it, Why you son of a bitch.

He reached and rang the buzzer but he never did quit looking at me. When the nurse come on and asked him what did he want he said something to make him sleep. She said well, it wasn't time for no sleeping shot, it was more like time for lunch. He mashed that button again.

When she answered that time he told her if he didn't have a shot in him to make him sleep in two minutes he was fixing to get up and kick somebody's ass.

About a minute later one come in there and told him to roll over. She raised his nightgown and popped him in the ass with a needle. Pulled his gown down and rolled him back over. Then she left. He was still looking at me.

He said You son of a bitch, and then closed his eyes.

What the hell does he mean talking that kind of shit to me. Like I ain't got enough on my mind already, don't know what the hell happened, where everybody's at, where's Beth, did I know what he wanted with a goddamn bayonet. James Earl Jones. Be damned if I'll drink any more of his damn beer. Where the hell's he even getting it anyway. You can't have that shit in a VA hospital. Damn I need to piss but I think I'll just lay here a minute and then get up later and go do it. I bet I'm either in Montgomery, Alabama, or Memphis, Tennessee, one. Ought to go down and visit the nut ward, see if I can find old Sherman. See if his ass is still in the can. Crazy son of a gun.

Like to never got him off that ledge. Would have splattered his brains all over those concrete steps. Just had all he could take. Two tours and two women. A twenty-one-year-old alcoholic. Boy he could pour that shit down. Probably kicked him out with a bad discharge. Just a zombie in a room with a U.S. Government robe on. Didn't even know us. They had him tranked out probably. We don't want you to hurt yourself or nobody else. Especially not none of us. Waste of a good man. Waste of a lot of good men. Boy I need to piss. Believe I'll get up and go in just a minute. So sleepy though. Sweepy sweepy. Get me one of them bedpans. Call that nurse. Ma'am, would you come in here and hold my penis while I urinate? My member? You remember my member? And would you bring a long piece of surgical tubing so I can suck some suds without having to get up? Not have to move? Lay here and watch a movie. Old Gregory Peck or somebody. James Earl Jones. You better get up and go piss if you're going to. If you're going to.

Well, after they stuck that shit in him it was all over with. I put too much on him too soon. Ought to knowed he was under a lot of stress. Couldn't even talk to him then. Couldn't do nothing but lay there and look at him.

They take your arms and legs you can't do nothing. Ain't no existence for a man. Noticed he never said nigger. Don't think it was in his vocabulary. He didn't even say black son of a bitch. Just son of a bitch. Which made me think he was too good a man. But I knew it would take a very good man. Done told him I wished I was dead. So it wasn't like it was unexpected. Just tried to lay it on him too soon.

Didn't know how long he'd stay out this time. Didn't know how much they'd shot him with. Usually they give em enough to keep em down about four hours. That's for a average-sized man. Somebody like him, somebody that big would more than likely have to have more. Like drinking. Goes by weight, not by size.

Laid there all day. They come in and fed me lunch and supper. Figured they'd slap the glucose to him but they didn't.

I didn't go nowhere. Thought about Jesus some. How anybody could be so mean to Him as to drive nails through Him. Them Romans was some sorry motherfuckers. No wonder all them volcanoes blowed up on em. You don't think the Lord made that happen? Shit. He punished them people for years. Burnt em alive.

Diva finally come in about dark. Brought some more beer and ice. Sat down and talked to me for a while. I told her what all happened. She said Well you just in too big a hurry. Trying to lay too much on him at one time. Say he all confused anyway, don't even know what he gonna do himself. Said you gonna have to take it easy on him. She looked over at him. Wonder what he looked like before his face got all messed up, she said.

Said she wanted to tell him what happened but she just couldn't do it. Looked at me. Hadn't been for you I woulda, she said. He don't need to be in here. He done had enough happen to him. He don't even know what all done happened to him. Then she started crying.

I asked her how many times had I done told her not

to be crying in here with me? She said she wasn't crying over me. I said Then what the hell you crying over? Him? She just looked at him. Then she started crying again.

Hell. Women. Can't do nothing with em. Half the time they won't even tell you what they crying over. And you just have to lay there and listen to it. It or the TV one.

She finally quit. But she was acting strange. Kept looking at him like she knowed something I didn't. I asked her did she bring us anything to smoke. She said yeah but it wasn't no need in her giving it to me now. He don't need it nohow, she said. And she said What you mean giving him that beer to drink? Said Don't you know that's bad for him? Said that was probably the reason he was in here right now, drinking too much with that head injury he had. Said Why don't you think about somebody besides yourself once in a while?

I said What the hell you going off on me for? I said the man wanted a beer, I give him one. Well don't be giving him no more, she said. I said How in the hell do you know what's wrong with him? She said Cause I done looked at his chart. Said he was on phenobarbital and wasn't supposed to drink nothing.

I said What time'd you get in last night? She said None of your business. I said yeah I knew what she was doing. Probably shacked up with somebody. I told her she better watch who she was messing with. Told her it wasn't like it used to be. And she just sulled up then. Don't like me telling her what to do.

It made her get off my ass about giving him the beer, though.

She kept on looking at him. I said You want that white man? She said I don't want nothing from him. You the one wanting something from him, she said. Then she got all huffy and left.

Left the beer, though.

After it got dark he was still out. Laying in his bed like a log. Thought maybe they'd done put too much in him. And then he might have been just laying there like he was asleep. He didn't move, though. I watched him. Wasn't no wonder he got hot. Hated I asked him about that bayonet stuff then. Wanted to hear about that woman. That girl. I couldn't figure out why she'd want to mess with him. I mean, I know that sound bad, but his face was a mess. I mean I ain't exactly no social celebrity myself. But at least I got a face. May be all I got. He didn't even have that, hardly.

Got too dark to see him good finally. They don't leave no lights on in here much. They just turn on a little one if they need it. They don't hardly ever need it. Ain't nobody in here going to get any worse than they already is.

I thought about going somewhere. But that get old too. Done about wore my imagination out going places. And wasn't sleepy. Wanted him to talk some more. Wanted Diva to come back and let my mind free.

Must've dozed off. Come to and the window was open behind me. Didn't hear her. Just felt her. Standing behind me. Walter was lighting a cigarette. I looked up backward and she kind of leant over and she was looking at me upside down and I was looking at her upside down. I said What the hell y'all doing? She said It's about time you woke up. We done had us a nice talk. And then she gimme a drag off that joint they'd been smoking. Had done about smoked the whole thing. Wasn't nothing but a roach left. Pissed me off. And what had they been talking about while I was asleep?

My name Diva.

Ever known what was happening around you while you were asleep? Think back. To a time you dreamed you were about to be awakened by somebody and then you were. It was like that. Kind of.

There was the humming first. A melody that crept into my hearing gradually. I knew it. I'd heard it before, lots of times, but I couldn't recognize it at first.

I felt her hands on me. They were warm and they felt like hands that could heal. She was humming the song. The one who had her hands on me.

I opened my eyes and looked at her. I guess I'd had a

nightmare. I was hot. I'd kicked some of the sheets off.

"Hey hon," she said. A fine-looking sister. Built. Medium fro.

"Hey," I said.

I was about to die to piss. I got up and did that, laid back down.

She put a hand on my forehead and felt of me. The hand was soft. It felt good.

"You all sweaty," she said. "Let me get me some cool water and I'll bave your face. Your face had a hard time, hon."

She stepped around to a sink somewhere behind me and I heard her running the water. I couldn't remember what I'd been dreaming, but it must have been a memory from when I was little and working in the field. I knew the song then. She came back with the washcloth and started cooling my face off, humming the song again. The pickers used to sing it. I'd never learned the words but I remembered the melody. Sometimes they sang it all day, and I used to listen to it all day. It was an old song, it had to be ancient, they must have brought it over on the ships. Maybe they sang it to keep themselves going. Maybe they sang it when they were chained flat on their backs in the hold. Crossing the ocean, leaving Africa, coming to a new world.

"Where'd you learn that song?" I said.

"Known that all my life," she said. "So you one of them Missippi boys, huh?"

"Nothing but."

Braiden was asleep. He was snoring. It sort of reminded me of a D9 Cat idling.

She finished what she was doing with me and pulled up a chair and sat down beside my bed.

"You had you a good nap," she said.

"Yeah. I asked for it."

She looked around some and then she pulled something out of her pocket and snapped a lighter and I saw while she had her face bent down to it that it was a joint. Then I smelled it. I looked around. I mean, hell, right in the middle of a fucking hospital. But all the lights were off. Nobody was stirring. She didn't seem to be worried about it anyway. When I looked at her again she wasn't even smoking it. She was just holding it out to me.

It wasn't very good. Some of that old cowshit homegrown. I guess it was the best they could do. I smoked it anyway. I sneaked looks at her tits once in a while. They were pretty awesome.

"You don't behave yourself you ain't never getting out of here," she said.

"What they gonna do?" I said. "Give me a prefrontal lobotomy?"

"They might."

I laughed a little.

She just said it again. "They might. You don't know what you messing with when you start messing with these doctors. They got documents they can sign. They got things they can do to you. You don't know. I'm a nurse. I work here. You better calm down."

I could just barely see her eyes. She was mostly just dark except for her white uniform. Her white cap was sort of riding in the air. The dope made her seem almost invisible.

"What's the matter with him?" I said.

"Who?"

"Him."

"Oh. Crazy. Maybe not crazy. Lay here long as he has, you might be crazy, too."

"Has he really been here that long?"

"He the oldest one here in this ward. He been here longer than anybody. They was an old fella from Korea but he died a while back. Braiden the oldest one here now." She paused for a second. "Wouldn't you be sick of it, too?"

I smoked some more of the joint. It wasn't bad once you got past that cowshit taste. I was starting to get a buzz. "I guess," I said.

"What did you and him have a falling out over?" she said.

I didn't want to tell her. I liked her right away. She wanted to be kind, but she had a hard side, too. I could tell. I knew she had to be that way. I knew this place would make you that way. But what nurse would bring in beer to the patients? Grass?

"I just didn't like the way the conversation was heading," I said. "He got to talking about some shit I didn't want to talk about. So I asked for a shot so I could sleep."

"Like what shit?"

She was sitting there in the chair with her legs crossed, watching me. I had the feeling that she knew something about me that I didn't know, and I couldn't figure out what it could be.

"Why are you fucking with my head?" I said.

"Ain't messing with your head. You think better when you smoke that stuff?"

"Sometimes."

"How long you been on phenobarbital?"

"I don't know. A while."

"How come them to take you off Dilantin?"

"Who you been talking to?"

"Doctors here and there. I read your chart. How come they took you off Dilantin?"

I looked away. "It wasn't controlling my seizures," I said.

"How much you drink?"

"None of your fucking business."

So she knew about the drinking. She probably knew everything. But I didn't. I looked at her again.

"You know what happened to me?"

"Yeah."

"You see this face I'm carrying around?"

"Yeah. So what?"

"So if I feel like drinking I don't want anybody to tell me I can't."

She hushed for about two beats. But I knew she was coming right back with something. She leaned a little closer first.

"That don't give you the right to kill yourself," she said.

"Why don't you tell him that, too? That's what he was talking about a while ago."

"He talks about a lot of stuff. He tell you about his trips?"

"What trips?"

"I mean the trips he takes in his mind. That's how he deals with it."

"Well," I said. "We all got to deal with it. I drink. And I ain't dead yet."

"You may be if you keep on. That grass ain't hurting you as bad as beer and whiskey is."

"I know all about that shit. What the hell you expect me to do? I can't get a fucking job. I can't drive a car. What the hell did they bring me here for anyway?"

She looked away.

"You had a bad seizure," she said.

"Well no screaming shit. I figured that."

I didn't know why I was being so hard on her. But goddamn it, I've *talked* to all those doctors. I *know* what the problem is. They want to cut on me, but they *don't* want to cut on me. Because that's where your talking is. One little slip with that knife . . . (after they've got the whole top of your head lifted off) and you don't talk no more. Hell. I don't talk to many people now.

"Look," I said. "I've been living with this for a long time. I take my medicine most of the time. I mean, I don't like it. It makes me feel strange. I mean that just makes it worse. All it does is just make me feel sorry for myself and want a drink. And then usually I take one. Jesus. Why don't you just go off and leave me alone?"

I had a buzz but it wasn't doing me any good. Not with her digging at me. I guess she saw it. She sighed. She got out of the chair and bent over me, straightening the sheet, tucking it in around my toes.

She stopped and put a hand on each side of me and leaned over so that her face was close to mine. I could see her up close then, her dark lashes, the whites of her eyes. She was a wet dream come true.

She lowered her face to me and kissed me, softly, once, on the mouth.

"Try to be patient with him," she said, and she took the burning joint out of my fingers. She went to stand behind his bed, and when she did, he woke up.

I looked at her, and I looked at him. I felt bad about calling him a son of a bitch. I thought about twenty-two years.

Baby that's a long, long long, long long long long time.

"You decided you'd wake up, huh? Ah hell we're just talking.

"Hey, man, I'm sorry. I didn't mean to go off like that. I've just got a lot of shit on my mind. Waking up in here and all. I thought somebody would have come to see about me by now. Or called. I just been drinking too much. That's all it is. I know better.

"You leaving? Oh. Okay.

"Man. How does she keep from getting caught? Hell, this dope. That beer. She takes good care of you, doesn't she? She said you were the oldest. I guess that's why.

"Yeah, I'll drink one. You sure you got plenty?

"Damn. I guess I'm just a rude sumbitch, ain't I? I haven't even asked you if you wanted me to hold one for you. Hell, I'm sorry. Naw it ain't all right. You're furnishing all the beer and I'm drinking it all up. Well shit. I'm new at this. What does she do? Sit on your bed? I mean I guess she does this for you, too, doesn't she? Well. I figured she did.

"Is that okay? Hell I'm not queer or anything. I'm not gonna mess with your genitals. Where can I put this cap? I think there's a pocket on this thing. Yeah. All right. You want a cigarette? Let me lean over here and get my lighter.

"Boy, that beer's cold, ain't it? I don't mean boy like boy. Sure. I know you do. I just feel like an asshole for acting like I did. I hope I'll get out of here tomorrow maybe. I don't think they really want to operate on me. It's too risky. God, I hate hospitals. I've spent so much time in them already.

"Here. How much? Hold it. Okay. You got a little on your chin there. Try to be a little neater. I'm just fucking with you. You don't care, do you? You were a pretty big man before this happened, weren't you? You've got a big chest. You ever lift any weights? You look like it. You must eat a lot. Just tell me when you want a drag off this cigarette. I'll get me one in a minute. I'll put some more beer in that cooler after while. We don't want to run out of cold ones.

"What about artificial limbs? Tried them, huh? Hell, what about a wheelchair you could operate? You've already tried all that shit, huh?

"Man does anybody ever take you outside? Let you look around? Aw man it's nice outside. The woods are full of green leaves. They were the other night.

"Aw shit, you don't want to hear all that. I don't even know what happened anyway. I guess I had a bad seizure or something and she had to call an ambulance. I guess that's how I wound up here.

"Did you catch a buzz? I did too. I'm talking my ass off I know. Usually I don't have anybody to talk to, though. Hell, I don't want to go in there and talk to Mama while I'm drunk. I write her letters sometimes, though. That's crazy as hell, ain't it? I'll write her a letter every once in a while and slide it under her door. And hell, she'll answer it like that. I don't know what I'm gonna do with her. Can't stick her in a rest home, she's not even sick. I wouldn't stick my mama in a rest home anyway. Oh. Your mama was in a rest home? Well hell. You couldn't take care of her, though. Your mama's been dead a month? I'm sorry to hear that she passed away, man. Did you get to go? Well. That's good that your sister takes care of you like that. You got any brothers? Five? Man. Y'all had a big family.

"I went to a funeral in a black church one time. I never will forget it. This old man lived on our place one time. His name was Hugh Jean. Shit, he used to cut my hair. Damn I ain't thought about Hugh Jean in a while. A mule kicked him in the head and killed him. Hell, I bet I wasn't but about twelve or thirteen. Daddy still had a couple of mules then. Hugh Jean raised him a garden with them every year. We had one that was an old mule. I mean that son of a bitch was old. Had white hair on his face. He was blind in one eye. Called him Joe. Daddy killed him after he kicked Hugh Jean in the head.

"Holler when you get ready for another beer. Yeah, hell. Old Hugh Jean used to tell me, Now son, you listen to me. You can plow behind one of these old mules for twenty years and he'll never try nothing. But the first time you bend over behind him and he knows it, he'll kick your head off. And damned if that wasn't what happened. This was after Daddy got out the first time. Hell, we never did know what happened exactly. It was one Saturday Hugh Jean was supposed to come up to the house and help Daddy plant some corn and he never did show up. He'd told Daddy he was going to break his garden up with old Joe and he'd be on up to the house quick as he got through. Well, hell, he never did show up. Daddy kept waiting on him. We had the planters on and the fertilizer loaded up. Finally he said, Well damn, surely to God he ain't drunk on a Saturday morning. So he went down there to see about him.

"Hugh Jean had a wife one time. I think her name was Sally. I don't even remember her. Hugh Jean killed her one Saturday night, Daddy said. With a razor. He went to the pen a long time before Daddy did. Got out after he did. Same crime I guess of a different color. Man how come y'all like knives so much?

"But he didn't have anybody else by then. Daddy and Mama let him move on the place to help. Daddy'd been knowing him a long time. He was pretty old then. He just lived by himself. He'd get drunk on the weekends and cry for Sally. No telling how long she'd been dead then. Say Lord send her back. Hugh Jean'll take care of her this time Lord if you'll just send her back. Mama couldn't stand it. She didn't want us around him when he was drinking. Boy you can remember a lot of stuff when you get to thinking about it. You sure can. Man I remember so much from back then.

"Here, let me get you another beer. This is nice, just us talking. Well. He was dead when Daddy found him. I walked close enough to see a little and then he made me go back. I kept watching, though. He was down on his knees by the front of the plow like he was working on it, Hugh Jean was. Old Joe was still standing in the traces. They'd broke up about half the garden. He didn't raise much. Some tomatoes and a few peas. A little okry. Enough stuff to get him through the winter. Hell, we raised hogs back then. Daddy and Hugh Jean did. I don't know, man. It was like they took care of each other. Daddy would go down there on the weekends sometimes and drink with him. He made a little whiskey down there. Mama didn't like that either. She thought it was going to get Daddy back in trouble again. But they never did get caught making it. Hell I make a little once in a while myself. I run me off a little batch once or twice a year, make enough to last me a while. I used to sit up in the woods with Hugh Jean and watch it come out a drop at a time. He taught me how to make it. Daddy knew he was doing it. I've thought about that a lot. He had a certain kind of relationship with Hugh Jean, and after he died it seemed like things were never the same. I don't know why. He never would let any black people live on the place after that.

"What he did was beat that fucking mule to death. Yep. Saw my daddy do that. God. He pulled Hugh Jean out of the way and took his shirt off and covered his face up. And I heard him talking to that mule. Said You son of a bitch I'm fixing to beat your fucking brains out. Oh he hurt that son of a bitch before he died. Took a sledgehammer handle to him. I saw some bad shit over there but my daddy beating that mule to death was one of the worst things I ever saw. It took him about thirty minutes. Mama got Max and ran in the house and locked the door. I stood there and watched it. He made sure the sumbitch suffered before he died. And he damn sure suffered. Tied his head to a post and then he went to work on him. He had blood all over him when he come back.

"This is some morbid shit, ain't it? Well hell. The mule killed his friend, so he killed the mule. But slowly, so the mule would know why it was happening. Not that you would have ever got him to admit that Hugh Jean was his friend. Hell no. The best he ever said was that Hugh Jean was a good hand.

"But I remember that funeral. Me and Daddy were the only white people in there. It was so strange. They didn't bury him for a week. They had to wait and let all his kinfolks from up North get down. They wouldn't bury him until everybody was there. What am I telling you for, hell, you know.

"Yeah, hold on, let me get my lighter. Here. You ready for a drink? All right.

"Naw but you know, Daddy wanted me to go. He said I might not get to see anything like that again ever. I didn't know what he was talking about.

"It was way up in the woods. This little dirt road, muddy, shit it'd been raining and cars were stuck everywhere. Hell, they had to get out and push the hearse out of a mud hole. And got up there and the church wasn't nothing but a little old shack, looked like. It was packed full of people. Every pew was jammed. They had to start putting chairs out in the middle aisle.

"Well, we got in there and sat down. Everybody was looking at us. I was afraid they's gonna kill us.

"A bunch of old women came in from the back, had choir robes on. Some of em looked like they were about eighty years old. I ain't shitting you, the most dried-up ones there, that was the ones in the choir. The ones who looked like they didn't have nothing left. Remind me to tell you the one about the piccolo player after while. But anyway they started singing. They didn't even have any music yet. The piano player hadn't even sat down yet. And hell, they didn't need it. They didn't even have any songbooks. They were just sitting there with their hands in their laps. But it made the hair want to get up on my head. I never heard nothing like it. They sang like angels. I mean, I've thought before, if you could hear angels sing, that's what it would sound like. They fit together like, well, it was like if one of them was gone it would have been something different. I mean you could hear every one of them. And nobody said anything, man, they just let them sing. I think they sang three songs, and I'd never heard a one of them before, but, man, God, I wish I had a tape of that now. I'd love to be able to hear that now, just one more time. Does that sound crazy? I mean I don't know how religious you are. But it was like God was up there in the rafters.

"I don't go to church like I ought to. I usually don't talk about any of this stuff. I don't know if they want to operate on me this time or not. It's risky.

"I was gonna finish telling you about that funeral. Well, the preacher came in. Man, it was hot in there. Wasn't any air conditioning, of course. He was a little old bitty guy with this long black robe. Had glasses. Kind of reminded me of Algonquin J. Calhoun. And he went to preaching. Then he got to preaching and singing. Then he went to hollering. And the whole place got to rocking and rolling. People were hopping up hollering Amen! like they just couldn't sit still. Then they went to testifying. The whole thing just got out of hand. It took about an hour. Everybody in there was sweating. I'd never seen anything like it.

"They opened the casket after it was all over with. The smell was awful. I think that's when death really hit me for the first time. We looked at him for a minute. Old Hugh Jean.

"That joke I was gonna tell you. They were having preaching one Sunday morning in this black church and they had a new piccolo player playing along with the choir. Well, they played two or three songs there and somebody all of a sudden hollered out in this real deep voice, The piccolo player's a motherfucker. Everybody hushed. The old reverend was up in the pulpit and he looked out over the congregation. He was just shocked. He said, Who was that called my piccolo player a motherfucker? Nobody said a word. Everybody was looking around to see who it was. The old reverend stood up there for a minute. Said, All right. I want the man who's setting next to the man who called my piccolo player a motherfucker to stand up. Nobody said a word. The old reverend was just getting madder all the time. He said, All right. I want the man who's setting next to the man who's setting next to the man who called my piccolo player a motherfucker to stand up. And hell, nobody stood up. Nobody said a word. The old reverend stood up there and just got pissed off as hell. Then he hollered, All right! I want the man who's setting next to the man who's setting next to the man who's setting next to the man who called my piccolo player a motherfucker to stand up! Finally there was this one little bitty guy in the back who stood up. And everybody was looking at him. He said, Reveren, I ain't the man who's setting next to the man who's setting next to the man who's setting next to the man who called your piccolo player a motherfucker. I ain't even the man who's setting next to the man who's setting next to the man who called your piccolo player a motherfucker. And I ain't the man who *called* your piccolo player a motherfucker. What I want to know is, who called that motherfucker a piccolo player?"

Well, hell, I'd heard it before. Didn't want to tell him that. Just laughed like I hadn't. He was talking to me and I didn't want to mess up no more. That beer was cold and we was laughing and drinking it and I had somebody setting on my bed talking to me, and you know, it was *nice* to have some company. It was so easy to just lay there and tell him to keep helping himself, and listen to him, and get a sip once in a while. Diva had been taking care of me, understand, but this was somebody different. Had a different life. Lived in a different place. His own world outside this one.

Shit, he could talk about movies, man, he knew them

actors. He could tell you the whole story of a movie, who was in it, what they said. But I knowed before the night was over I was gonna have to ask him again about *The Young Lions*. Cause it wasn't no other way out. Cause nice as it was right then, it wasn't going to last. Sun was gonna come up again. And I'd be laying here with no place to go. I was tired to my soul, Jesus, hope You understand. And be merciful. Hope You was merciful to Hugh Jean, whoever he was. Might've bent over behind that mule on purpose. Might've been toting too much pain. A man can get more than he can tote. You know that. Didn't You ask for the cup to pass on? And I'm sorry for what they done to You. Wish I'd been there to help You. I'd have laid em to waste. Put em to the sword. But Your will be done.

"You got a clock around this place? Where? This drawer here? Let me see. Twenty after two. You sleepy? Me neither. Don't they ever come in here and check on you at night? Hell, we'll just lay down if we see somebody come in. Make out like we're asleep.

"Is Diva working now? She gonna come back by and see you before she leaves? Man, she's good-looking. She ought to be in *Playboy* or something.

"Ah shit, you don't want to hear all my problems. Probably just make you more depressed than you already are. How do I know?

"Well goddamn. You were talking about killing yourself, weren't you? You ain't got any way to do it even if you really wanted to.

"I don't know what you'd do, man. Hell, Braiden. You sound like Mama.

"Nah, hell, I don't think they saw me. I don't think they were up yet. I don't guess Mama sleeps much. But her room's on the back side of the house anyway. I just climbed back in through my window and went to sleep. It was so hot I had to turn the air conditioner on. I can't sleep in that heat. Gives me nightmares.

"What surprised me was her coming back to see me. I was going to watch a movie. I got up late that evening and opened a beer. I drank about half of it. Next thing I knew, somebody was knocking on the window and it was dark. I'd had another spell and I didn't even know it. I didn't even know it was her at first. Kind of like when I woke up in here. It took me a minute to figure out what was happening. It always does. Usually I wake up on the floor. Or the side of the road. Or a car where somebody's left me. I've been robbed outside bars like that before. Motherfuckers have done that to me too.

"I guess Max and Mama were gone. He takes her down to this catfish place down the road sometimes. I got up and went to the window and said who was it and it was her. I'm always confused when I wake up. It takes me a few seconds to adjust. And I just had on my underwear anyway. I had to put some pants on. She said she'd come to see me. So I went over and pushed open the screen. I felt like a dilbert, of course. It's a real low window. It's easy to get in and out of. She had a big sackful of beer with her. I set that on the floor and then helped her on in.

"You'd have to see my room to understand this. It's just a damn big mess. I've got books all over the place and movie posters. I've got a bunch I sent off for from back in the sixties. A bunch of psychedelic posters and stuff. She just stood there and looked at everything for a minute. We had a combat photographer with us for about a month. He was working for *Life*. He made a bunch of pictures of us and I've got some of them on the wall. They're all of the way I looked before. Before I got hit. One of them I'm crossing this river with the M60 over my head, keeping it dry. And he was with us the day I got shot the first time. I've got blood all over me, and the guys loading me in the chopper have got blood all over them. Everybody's screaming. The gunners are laying about a thousand rounds a minute out the doors. It's a hell of a photograph. Anyway she stood in front of it for a long time and looked at it. Then she finally asked who that was they were putting on that helicopter. I said that was me. I said that was what I used to look like.

"She touched the picture, touched my face on it. I asked her how she knew which room was mine and she said she'd watched me that morning when I went in. I told her to sit down and we got us a beer out. She laid down on the bed over there. She said she'd been kind of afraid to come up to the house. Said she didn't know if we had any dogs or not. I told her that we hadn't had a dog in a long time, that we couldn't keep one there, that they kept getting run over, so close to the highway and all. She said well she was glad of that because she hated dogs. Said she got bit real bad by one when she was little. And I still didn't know. This was before we really got to talking.

"I asked her something else about it and she said yeah, a dog got ahold of her when she was five and almost killed her. Said she had scars all over her, all under her clothes. I told her I couldn't see any. She didn't say anything for a little bit. Then finally she said she couldn't wear shorts. Couldn't wear a swimming suit. Said she didn't want anybody to see her legs.

"I told her I was sorry. Hell, I didn't know what to say.

"She said that was okay, that she was just glad he didn't kill her. That he almost did.

"She got up and went over to the bookshelves and started looking at my books. I've got a bunch of them. She asked me if I'd read all of them. I told her yeah. She said she wished she liked to read. And I couldn't understand that. I told her that I thought the more you read, the more you wanted to read. She missed so much school when she was little, she never did learn to read very well. She was in the hospital a lot. You know, having operations. Plastic surgery and all. She said she missed so much, she never could catch up, so she just quit.

"I hated it. What are you supposed to say? She turned around and told me she knew what I felt like. Said her mama couldn't stand to even look at her after that dog got ahold of her.

"I told her it took my mama and them a long time to

get used to me. That I didn't really know if they ever had or not. She wanted to know if I ever felt sorry for myself. She said she used to, but she didn't anymore. Said it was a waste. And then she asked me again. I mean she really wanted to know.

"Hell, I thought about it. I told her that I'd accepted it the first time I looked in a mirror in the Philippines. Which I think I did. I knew I'd never look right again. I knew the face I'd been born with was gone. And nothing was going to bring it back. Oh hell, I've felt sorry for myself plenty of times. But I've always known nothing was going to bring it back.

"Hell, look at you. I'd bet a million dollars you don't feel sorry for yourself. And I'd bet another million that one time you used to. Am I right?

"Get you another drink, bro.

"I don't reckon she got in any trouble about the store being closed. She went back and made some coffee and then Earl came in about seven and let her off. He didn't know it had been closed.

"We talked for a while. And then out of the blue she just asked me to kiss her. No shit. I told her I hadn't kissed anybody in a long time. She said that didn't matter, and what I looked like didn't matter, and that she'd show me what she meant sometime.

"She was so . . . innocent, seemed like. I laid down beside her on the bed. And I was afraid she was too young. She touched my face, all these messed-up places. She wasn't scared. It was like she understood. She kissed me.

And I'll be damned if Max and Mama didn't drive up right that minute and come in the house.

"I was nervous as hell anyway. I didn't know what was going to happen and I didn't want them to hear us. Hell, I can have a movie playing sometimes and hear one of them come down the hall. They don't think I can hear them since a movie's on, see. But I can. And they'll stop right beside the door and listen. Wondering what I'm doing. I just didn't want to have her in the house while they were there. I didn't want them to hear us talking or anything. I mean we weren't doing anything. But I didn't have anyplace else to take her. I mean we were doing a *little* stuff, but not, you know. Well, I guess we were kind of headed in that direction. And shit, man, I didn't even know for sure how old she was. I felt kind of like a pervert. It wasn't dirty or anything. It's hard to explain. I wish I could say what I mean. She moved something in me. I don't give the time to most people. Most people just look at me and see one thing. I mean I know I've gotten hardened and all, but it's like it's a defense mechanism. When you go somewhere . . . where do you go? Africa? Africa. Well. You've had to do that to keep from going crazy, right? Hell, I know where you're coming from. You can't lay here and look at these four walls. I bet they keep that television on all day long, don't they? God, I hate television. PBS is all I watch, man. No shit.

"But what I was telling you. I see people, man, and I know they see me. But they don't see *in* me. They see this fucked-up face, and that's it. I mean I don't stay in the house twenty-four hours a day. And I don't shun my family completely. I spend some time with them. But if I get ready to be by myself, that's what I do. And if I get ready to go somewhere, I go. I guess I just like being out at night because I don't have to deal with many people. The ones I deal with see me over and over. They're used to me. Like Earl. They don't think anything about me. And that was what was so hard to understand about her. Anyway. I didn't want us to stay there after they came in. So I said Hell, let's take the beer and go riding around somewhere. I told her I'd put some gas in her car. I didn't want to have to explain everything about me and my mother and my brother there. Or my daddy. I just wanted to be off with her. Nobody else. Just us two. So she said fine. I told her I had a quilt. We just got my cooler and put the beer in it and got the quilt and eased out the window.

"Damn, man, watch it, here comes a nurse. Let me hop my ass back in bed a minute."

I didn't make no noise. I wanted him to talk to her. Wanted to hear what was said. She knowed I was awake. She could tell.

It was late. Don't know what time. You can tell by the traffic. Slows down late at night. Hear them sirens way off, fire trucks, police cars. Ambulances. People in trouble all over the city. Other people trying to help them. Everything outside is yellow at night, just a yellow glow. Them lights they turn on, I guess. Helicopter got to see how to land. Heard one of them come in, just chopping that air. Brought back some bad memories.

May be some in here that sleep, but this place don't never. Always somebody hurt. Always somebody need taking care of. But it was mostly quiet. You could hear that, too. And them talking.

Hell, it was her. I could hear her nylons swishing before I could even see her. Thighs rubbing together. Small sounds of erotica for somebody who does without.

I guess Braiden had crashed. Bored him to sleep, I guess. I spoke to him but he didn't answer. I said something else to him and she told me not to make so much noise.

She said, "You ain't drunk, are you?"

I said naw. Had a few beers was all. Little smoke.

"Well he's asleep," she said. "Don't mess with him."

I asked her if she wanted a beer.

"How's your head feeling?" she said.

I told her I thought it was all right for the moment, but I didn't know how long it would last. I told her I thought I might swoon just any time.

"I'll revive you."

She sort of had her hand laying there on my leg. What the hell, I wasn't feeling any pain. Not a whole lot. I mean I was feeling *some* pain, but damn, we all feeling *some* pain.

I asked her what her doctors wanted to do about my head.

"They don't know," she said. "They ain't decided nothing. They may not do nothing to you. Just let you go on back home."

All this time she was tucking in my sheet and shit. I laid there and thought about it. That was all I wanted, to go home.

"If you'd take your medicine like you supposed to and cut down on your drinking you'd be all right," she said.

I told her I knew all that shit. Then she dropped her bomb on me.

"Your mama called," she said. She wasn't looking at me when she said it, but she took a deep breath. "You were out two days after they brought you here. Your family's been here. Your brother and your mama. Me and Max set out in the hall drinking coffee and talking about you. He said you been having these spells for a long time. Said back when they wanted to operate on you, you wouldn't let em. Is that right?"

I asked her how come she didn't tell me that my family had already been to see about me when she first talked to me.

"You wasn't in no shape to tell then. Besides. They was already gone when you woke up the first time."

I got my beer out from under the covers and finished it. Right away she got me another one. Right after telling me how bad they were for me. But it was cold, and I wanted it, so I didn't say anything. Neither of us did for a little while. I lit another cigarette, and kept my voice calm, and asked her if she knew anything about somebody named Beth. That was when she sat down on the bed.

She turned her head away. Said she didn't know anything. Didn't know what had happened. All she knew was a helicopter came down and she unloaded it. That I'd had a bad seizure and they were trying to help me if I'd let them.

She had her legs up on the bed next to me. Fine, heavy, thick. Real legs.

"All I know's what they told me when you come in," she said.

I told her I wasn't trying to sound nasty or anything. But I'd just found out I'd been out for two days and nobody was telling me anything. I said *Christ!*

"She's gonna call back in the morning," she said.

That made me feel a little better. I looked over there at old Braiden. I couldn't tell if he was asleep or just making like a marsupial. She got up and started fluffing my pillow. Rubbed one of her big old titties right across my nose one time. Inadvertently, of course. I told her how good she smelled.

"What y'all been talking about?" she said.

"Just different stuff."

"Different stuff like what?"

"We've been talking about the movies," I said. "You going to wake him up? I don't believe he's asleep. You're not asleep, are you, Braiden?"

If he was asleep, he wasn't snoring.

"You got a boyfriend?"

"Not a steady one. Ain't got time for it."

"I bet he wishes you'd make time for it. What do you do that keeps you so busy?"

"Take care of him."

"All the time?"

"Just about. I come see him on weekends when I'm off. See if he needs anything."

She sat back down on the bed. It was quiet in there. I laid there sipping my beer. I knew there was plenty more.

"How much longer till daylight?" I said.

She got up and looked out the window, then looked down at me.

"Long time yet," she said. "Sometimes the nights are long in here. You know what I mean?"

"I thought nights were the same everywhere."

"Not quite," she said. She patted my leg one time and said she'd see me later. I just nodded. I was listening to her nylons again, the little swishes fading away with the white glow of her dress.

I didn't say nothing. Just kept laying there with my eyes closed. Didn't know how to begin again. Didn't want him to ask for another shot. I wanted him to stay awake and talk to me. Wanted him to get some more of that beer in him. Knowed it wasn't no problem. Just had to let him do a little thinking. Just thought I'd give him a little more time alone. See what we could come up with.

A answer, if there was one.

It was so easy to just lay there and drink beer. It was dark, and everybody was asleep, and nobody was going to catch me and take it away from me. Besides, I needed it. It was helping. But I was worried like hell.

The only thing I could figure out was that Beth got scared again when it happened. She probably had to go for help. Or maybe she just went on home after they got me. It had to be something like that. It was no major problem. Mama would call, and I'd tell her I was all right, and then they could come get me and I could go home. I was ready for some home.

I could explain everything to Max and Mama later. I

knew they were worried about me. Something like this happens, you can't help but worry. They'd already tried to talk me into having that operation. For years. And so much that I got tired of hearing it. I had a bad argument about it with Max one day. Here's one example of the asshole I can be. I told him I'd slap the shit out of him if he didn't shut up about it.

I'm a real nice guy.

Hell, all he was trying to do was help me. I passed out one day in the yard a while back and they like to never got me inside, they said. We were just out there looking at the garden. I'd told Mama I'd get out there that evening and hoe her peas and stuff. Then bam. Woke up at five o'clock the next morning, both of them on stools right next to the couch. Worried as hell. I just went on to my room. Didn't say shit. Hello goodbye kiss my ass or nothing. But *damn*.

They don't know how I feel. People can't tell you they know how you feel. Wear a face like this around for a while. See people cringe when they look at you. Then tell me you know how I feel. Start watching *Easy Rider* and wake up with snow on the screen. Then tell me you know how I feel. Max and them can't tell me what I need to do. Because I don't know what I need to do myself.

I don't guess I have to be such an asshole about it, though.

The way I look at it, I only have a few hours left. Mama will call back in the morning. I can talk to her and find out about Beth and tell her to send Max after me. I can stand it that long, surely.

I looked over at Braiden. Jesus, his arms. His legs. And twenty-two years on a bed. The shit just comes down and sometimes it lands on you. Or the guy next to you. If you're lucky, the guy next to you.

I got me another beer. I wasn't a bit sleepy. I knew I could make it till daylight. Till time to leave, if that's what they were going to let me do.

Then I thought: I can leave. He can't.

I was even promising myself that I'd come back and see him, knowing all the time it was a damn lie. I couldn't wait to get out of here. And I damn sure wasn't coming back unless it was flat on my back.

I didn't have any answers ready when he started talking to me again.

"Well. I see you still awake. Diva been in here? Aw. She done gone, huh?

"Naw, I don't think I want one right now. I might take one later. But you help yourself to all you want. Shit, man, I'm drawing a check, too. Got all kinds of money in the bank. I even got some CDs. It just goes in there and makes more money. Man. What I could do now if I could get up and around.

"Man, you think about it. I'm drawing pretty good money now. Don't even see it. It just goes into a draft. That old interest just piles up and piles up. Diva fixed it all up for me. She take care of all my stuff for me, my banking and all. It don't cost me nothing to stay in here. Government pays for that. Twenty-two years, man, it adds up. They ain't nothing I can do with it anyway. It ain't doing me no good. Ain't never going to spend none of it. Ain't got nothing to buy.

"Man, you take just a thousand dollars. Just say for a year. And just say seven percent interest. First year you got a thousand and seventy dollars. And you keep piling it up. And man in twenty-two years it done built up. That ain't no small loaf of bread. I get a statement every so often. It's a miracle what that money does when you let it stay in there. I had a guy come see me one day wanted me to invest in some stocks and bonds. I told him, Shit, I ain't fucking with no stocks and bonds. What I want to be risking my money for when it's insured where it is and making all that other money?

"This hadn't happened to me, I probably wouldn't have nothing. Houseful of kids. Working in some factory somewhere. House payments.

"I would have like to tried it, though. Just to see how it was. Yeah. Wife and kids. A whole family. Leg down every night if you want to. Supper on the table when you come in from work. Watch them younguns grow up."

"Hell, man. Diva said Mama called up here to talk to me. And they've *been* here. Her and Max. I can't figure out what's going on.

"I reckon it was while they had me knocked out. I wish to hell somebody would tell me something. I hope they let me out of here in the morning.

"I've got to cut down on my drinking. After tonight I will. I haven't been taking my medicine. I know I drank too much that night.

"We went up this old logging road. Got off the highway. I just wanted to talk to her. It wasn't very late. We got the quilt and spread it out and got the beer out of the car. She had us a couple of joints rolled up. So we smoked about half of one of them. The moon was out. It was nice, you know? I mean I haven't spent any time with a woman in so long.

"Hell, you know what I mean.

"Ache, yeah, right, you ache. Man. How you ache. I wanted to go slow. Be careful. I hadn't figured out what was going on yet.

"We messed around a little. Nothing heavy. It was nice just to be able to lay up next to her. We were so high, and everything was so slow. We just laid there and listened to it. There was all kinds of stuff to hear once you got to listening to it. You could hear cars way the hell off on the highway. Hear those tree frogs, and see like it was daylight.

"It's not like I'm telling the whole world or anything. I'm just telling you. Well, we got to messing around, and she unbuttoned her shirt. I think I told you she was built pretty good. And, man. Man.

"You ready for a beer now? Let me get you one. Hell, I might as well drink one, too. Remind me to put some more in there later. I'll just get up here on your bed again.

"There. I don't know how to explain it. I'll tell you what it was like, Braiden. It was like I was a baby. That's how it was. I felt more comfort, and more safety, and . . . *love,* than I've felt in a hell of a long time.

"I had a girl over there one time. Thought I was in love with her. I was gonna bring her back over here. Marry her. Have me some beautiful little black-headed kids. That's when I was new. Nobody told me. I mean you stay out on the line for a couple of months and then come back in and get a little time off and you go back to see her, right? What? Did I expect her to stay pure? With eight thousand other marines with money in their pockets? I guess I did. Me and a guy from California had a real bad little scrape over her. I mean with knives. And she wasn't even worth it. Just a whore.

"Beth wasn't like that. I was turned on to her. She looked good. It wasn't just a sexual thing. I mean, there was that, sure, but then it was something else too. And see, she'd already given me a hint. I just hadn't picked up on it. I should have known something, I guess. Hell, look at me. That should have told me something. I didn't know why, but I knew we fit together, that we belonged together. That's how I felt."

Yeah. *Fit* together. Lord didn't we fit together. It was better with her than it was with Sharon Neal all those nights in the back of the truck. Right in the middle of the cotton patch. In the cotton pen. Anyplace. Every place. God she's fat now. Huge. She was beautiful. Sixteen. Sweet sixteen.

"Well, Beth started asking me all these questions. And I would have told her anything. She wanted to know what happened to me. So hell, I told her. Started telling her. Just about that day, going over there looking for them people and getting hit and all, all the time I stayed in the hospital at Subic Bay, what the bullet did to me. How I passed out sometimes. I said that was what had happened the night before. And then again the next afternoon. That afternoon. I just told her the whole thing. And she listened, never said a word, just held me. Until I got through.

"Then she started talking in this real strange, quiet voice. Like what she was telling hadn't happened to her, but to somebody else. And I found out what happened, why I was with her, why she thought we were supposed to be together.

"She said they had this neighbor when she was little. And he had this big black Chow dog he kept in his back yard. She was scared of it. Wouldn't even go near the fence. It had these eyes, she said, with something crazy inside for her. But only for her. The damn thing just terrified her. I think she was five. And her aunt and some of her kinfolks came over one day and her mama carried them all in the house and left her out in the yard. She said her daddy had fixed her up a sandbox and she went around in the back yard and started playing in it. She didn't know whether he jumped the fence or what. She just heard something behind her and it was him. Said he didn't even growl or nothing. Just started biting her. He had her foot to start with. She kicked him and got up and tried to run, but he grabbed her in her back and pulled her down. Said it was a big dog. Probably weighed more than she did if she was only five. She tried to push him off with her hands. He bit every one of her fingers, both thumbs. And she was screaming the whole time but nobody heard her. They were all sitting in there with the air conditioner running. I don't know how long it went on. She said a long time. The dog had blood all over his head. Her blood. She said she guessed he would have killed her. But the garbagemen came up the driveway to get the garbage and saw her under him. She said she'd never forget that. She said this little short nigger man. Great big arms. He'd done bit her up and down both legs, all over her stomach. He'd bitten a bone in her left arm in two. And that guy ran up and grabbed him by the neck and pulled him off of her. He bit him one time, then the guy doubled up his fist and hit him between the eyes. They threw him down on the concrete and killed him with a shovel, she said. Beat him to death. And just kept on beating him. Stomped him. Just kept on stomping him. Which I guess it scared them. They probably thought she was dead. And I imagine she looked like she was. Hell, blood all over her. She lost almost three pints. Almost died. It's a wonder she didn't. Hell. A grown man will die from that sometimes. You've seen that. Shock and blood loss. I know I have. It could have gotten you, right? Sure. I mean you must have had some terrible damage. What? Did you have a corpsman tie everything off? That's probably what saved you. What saved me, a corpsman. I had pretty massive blood loss out of the top of my head. But they had blood on the chopper that came for me. I don't know how much they put through me. I had emergency surgery in a field hospital before they put me on the plane. I don't remember any of that shit. That's just what they told me.

"What were you hit with? AK? Well. It's a hell of a weapon.

"She said her daddy liked to killed the guy who had the

dog. They put him in jail over it. I didn't know what to say. We lit us a couple of cigarettes and just laid there and smoked for a while. She said she hated for me to see her legs but she guessed sometime I'd have to. She didn't think anybody would want her. That's what it was.

"Hell. What else could I do? I fastened her clothes back together. We got to talking about how one little thing could mess up your whole life. Just being in the wrong place at the wrong time. Same with me, same with her. Hell, man. Same with you.

"I mean you can't change that shit, though. I've thought about it. You can't change anything. She said her mama always thought God had punished her for things she'd done by letting that dog get ahold of her. Her mama died in Whitfield. Screaming about Jesus.

"She's caught a lot of shit not to be any older than she is.

"See, they came after her mama, to take her off, and her daddy was about half blind. He hid her in a laundry hamper when they came in the house and told her to be quiet. I don't know how old she was then. Probably seven or eight. He was afraid they'd take her, too. Thought he might be an unfit parent. She could remember hiding in that basket, hearing them come in after her mama, having to chase her down inside the house and all, her screaming and hollering all that crazy stuff, all that crazy shit. Some of this stuff, it was hard for her to tell me.

"I don't think her mother lived much longer. I don't know when all this was. It couldn't have been too many years ago.

"I've got to get back home and see her. She may not even know if I'm alive. I don't know if she talked to Mama or not. I don't know what's going on. I wish it would hurry up and get daylight. I'm ready to get out of here."

"I thought I was dead, Walter. I never had seen that much blood at one time. And all of it was coming out of me.

"Ambushed us. Done it just like ours taught us to do it to them. It was the first and last firefight I was ever in in the daytime. Usually you know it would be at night. I was wounded once before this. Down here on my leg, where my leg used to be. That part of it gone now. Some sumbitch shot me and me standing behind a tree. I ain't never figured out till yet how he done that. It wasn't no bad wound, though. I had a pretty good set of legs on me back then. It come in right down here, about six inches above my knee, went on out the back. It was just a small caliber rifle. But you know it was on the outside of my leg, down here in this thick muscle. It didn't hit a bone or nothing, it just went on out. Left a little hole about as big as your little finger. Didn't even bleed that bad really. This other, though. Man I like to bled to death. Like to died from shock. Lose that much blood, it shocks your whole system. Like you said while ago. If they hadn't had blood on the chopper that come for me, that'd been the end of me. And which it would have been a whole lot easier on everbody if it had. My mama took it hard. See, they didn't tell her I'd lost my arms and legs. They just said I had numerous injuries. And which they had done amputated everything as quick as they got my blood pressure back up. Hell, they couldn't do nothing else with me. I had two arteries wide open. And everything else, you know, they wasn't no saving it. They couldn't even tell exactly how many times I was shot. They estimated twenty rounds hit me. Might not have been that many. Might have been more. That's what my wounds was like. But them guys was used to dealing with that kind of stuff. Some of them doctors was doctors in World War II. I had one of them tell me, he used to talk to me all the time, come in there and set with me, he said he did surgery on several men who was shot with fifty-caliber bullets, and hell, they lived, some of em. You know it just depends on where you get hit.

"See, where I was at, and the way it happened, there wasn't nothing for me to get behind. We was going down this trail. I was on point. And you know what the point man's chance is in a ambush. What they done was let the last ones get on in. And we was spread out a little wider than they were so I was almost out of range when they started. Six men was dead in the first five seconds. But I was trying to get back. Help my guys out. Our machine gunner was dead. Mortarman was dead. Squadleader was dead and my fire team leader, too. Then they started laying mortars in on us. Bullets flying everywhere. The damn bushes was just jumping. It was a hell of a line of fire coming from the left flank. I had one of them converted M14s. Throwed her on auto and laid about three clips into his ass. Silenced that one. People was hollering all kinds of shit, you know how it is, and you couldn't stand up. They was this one old boy I used to drink beer with from Chicago, he was down and hollering for me. He died two days later, they said. And he was laying close to this little knoll but he was in the wide open. He wasn't moving, just hollering. And we was starting to drive them back. Somebody recovered the M60 and got the bipod down, and another guy got the ammo. They started killing some people then. Smoke, damn, you couldn't hardly breathe for the gunsmoke. But we had em down to about two guns then. Knew they's fixing to run. I raised up just a little to put another clip in and they hit me right here on my right arm. Didn't hit the bone. Tore a big hole in my bicep, though. And where I thought he was at, I thought he was down in front. Thought I could crawl up behind that little knoll and get Don. But the guy with the gun, he could see me. I started crawling to that little knoll and that's when he cut loose. I felt them bullets run up my legs, man, just punching holes in me. Couldn't move. Then he just raked me. Just all over. Lord he shot me all to pieces. Lord he hurt me.

"But I would have done it to him if he'd give me the opportunity. I remember the first one I killed. I was new in country. Had my little flak jacket and helmet on, so damn scared my teeth was rattling. And they put me in this platoon with a bunch of wooly boogers. I don't know how long it had been since they'd been out of the boonies. First day they said Well get your shit ready because we going out. Hell we took off and went out on a little patrol there, they had me back in the middle because I didn't know shit. Man we was snoopin' and poopin'. The recon had done been out and found some sign and snuck back, so we was looking. I just knew I was gonna get killed the very first day. I'd done said my prayers. I was steady talking to Jesus.

"Well they found em a tunnel. Snuck around there and looked and looked and found where it come out. About two hundred yards away. They had em a good rat so they carried me back and give me a .45 and set me down and said Now we fixing to go see if anybody's home and you set here and watch and if he comes out you blow his ass off. Then they just left me. I got down next to this tree and leaned back against it, had that pistol in both hands. Hadn't shot one since basic training. Had the safety off, had it aimed out there. Setting there shaking. Thinking

Lord what am I gonna do? Didn't know how long it would take. Hell. I was eighteen years old. I bet they hadn't been gone ten minutes. I heard something bump down there in the ground. And I said Oh shit. I took my helmet off. The hole wasn't but about twenty feet away. Well, this door come up, had grass and dirt and shit all over it, and I saw this black hair stick out. Just a little. Just had his eyes stuck up. Looking to see if anybody was waiting on him. But it opened away from me, see. Just luck I set down where I did. Behind him. And I knew he'd have to turn his whole head around and look behind him before he'd come on out. But I don't know why, he didn't do it. He kept that door pushed up for about a minute. Then there it come on up. And he come out. I guess he was in a hurry. Didn't know we'd found his exit. Thought it was all right, I guess. And I knew I was fixing to kill him. Had it right on him. He come out and set on the edge of that hole, had his legs hanging down in it. He looked up and seen me. Didn't try to do nothing. Just quit. I shot him one time in the chest and he just fell back. Just laid there. Dead as a hammer. It was just as quiet. Wasn't a sound. Like I killed everything when I killed him. I kept telling myself he wasn't gonna put his hands up and was fixing to reach for his weapon. What it was, I didn't give him a chance to do nothing. I was so scared I killed him before he could move.

"I felt bad about the first one. But it didn't last long. Not after I had been out there for about a month. We had a guy got lost one night out with us. Got separated from us during a firefight. We found him about three days later, wired to a tree. Yeah. I quit feeling bad then. That was the first time I saw what they did to us if they caught us. I made up my mind they wouldn't catch me alive. Always had me one round in my pocket for me. Yes sir."

"Would you have used it, though? Could you? Well. You can't ever tell. All the guys who were shot down, look how many of them were captured. Aw hell, I know they executed some of them. Maybe a lot of them. You oughta heard my daddy talk about that in the war. He wouldn't tell it unless he was drunk. But I've heard him tell it over and over and cry over it.

"He said they had this one guy in their platoon who liked to do it. Hell yeah. Kill em. Way he told it, when the push was on, they didn't have time to take any prisoners. They didn't hardly have time to eat. Hell, man, they did worse stuff than that to us. To the Jews. Look at the Japanese. They liked to chop heads off.

"Aw, he just said they had this guy in their platoon. He just told about this one day. The Germans were freezing, they didn't have any clothes. We'd broken all their supply lines. I guess this was near the end, when the German army was in rout. They had more prisoners than they could take care of. I guess he knew they had to do it. Your values are not the same then. You want to live, right? Sometimes for you to live, somebody else has got to die. But his life's not the same as yours then, is it? His life is less than yours, isn't it?

"I know where you been, man. I've decided it's all the same. It's just the places and the reasons that change. Or maybe just the enemy. Hell. Let's open us another beer.

"He knew about Leningrad, about them baking bread out of sawdust. They laid siege to it for over two years, the Germans did. It was something like a million starved to death. He knew the things that had gone on. But I guess he couldn't help but feel sorry for human beings. He said a lot of their prisoners didn't even have toes, man, they'd froze them off. Nothing to eat. And they would get down on their knees and hold out their hands asking for bread. But they couldn't keep them. They had to go on.

"He said there were fifteen or twenty that day. They'd held them since morning. And they were going to move out the next morning. They couldn't take anybody with them. So he said the guy with the machine gun told them all to stand up, that they were taking them to get fed. I guess some of them knew enough German to talk to them. And he marched them off into the woods. He said some of them threw down things. Cigarette lighters, pictures of their kids. Medals. They were jabbering, he said, he didn't know what they said. But they knew where they were going. He said not a one tried to run. Just kept their hands on their heads and went off with that guy. Off in the snow. He could still hear their feet. Crunching in the snow. Everybody was listening. He said it was quiet for a long time.

"Then the machine gun cut loose. He could hear them screaming.

"The war ruined my daddy as much as anything else. I mean his drinking and all. Mama never could figure that shit out. She always said it looked like after I'd seen what it did to him I wouldn't do it.

"Hell, I'm pretty bad to drink. I guess you can see that. I'm pretty bad to smoke that old shit, too. Life's so easy then, though. Just for little periods. Smoovo, you know? Smoove everything over. You got another joint in that drawer? Did she leave us another one? Well let's smoke that son of a bitch.

"Here. Hold on. I got a light right here. Just let me get this. That window still open? Okay. Here. Go to it, man. Get all you want. Cause we need to talk. You know how long it's been since I talked to anybody like this? I don't know where I'm gonna be tomorrow, right? My little brother was just a kid when I went off. And everything was so fucked up in the world.

"I'll smoke a little of it. Not much. I got to be straight when she calls. I got to get my shit together and get out of here. I've got to get ahold of Beth, man. I got to see her. You dig where I'm coming from, man? I know you do. I know you do."

Now he's in there, Bwana, and he's packing some American lead in his ass and not in too good a humor so which one do you want, the .475 Roberts-Schnauzer or the 82/40 Shootmaster with the double ivory grips? I'm telling you, Bwana, he's pissed off. Now you can get your white ass up a tree and let us beat the bushes and run him out or you can play the cool fool and come out needing about 967 stitches in your ass. Either way we fixing to bind him over cause we needing us some advance money. Now we having to put up tents which ain't even in our contract and I thought I'd speak to you personally but I didn't mean to pick a time like this. I mean, think about it, Bwana. We out here every day, we up before breakfast cooking impala liver and scrambling eggs and stuff and then we got to have all the dishes washed at night before we can even get us a rice beer. Now watch out there's a bent piece of grass right there. And see that blood right there? Look.

You got him, Bwana, come on.

What I was saying. See, we even having to tote luggage and shit. We all . . . did you hear something? Whole lotta blood right here. He probably done gone. Or behind us one. And man we working some late hours. I mean . . . look here. See that bright red? Lung blood. Ain't nothing to worry about, man, come on. You got the whole Remington Gunpowder Factory behind you. My daddy used to kill these things with a spear. Shit, he didn't get no pussy till he was like twenty-nine. They kept him out there in the tall grass. Made him watch the cows. Shit, man, he knowed Hemingway when he was over here. Aw, yeah, Papa and my papa was like this close. They used to go lion hunting every day. He said Hemingway thought they ought not shoot so many lions cause they had so many cows. Something he said about rich folks the same the world over. I never did understand all of it. I think they used to set around the fire at night and talk.

Was that twig moving just then?

You smell something?

Okay, Bwana. I see him. There he is. Damned if you didn't make a lousy shot on him. You don't see him? Shit, I see him. Hope he don't see us. There he is, right there.

Right there. *Naaaaaaw*, shit. Right there. See his leg laid out behind him? Now hell be quiet. You don't see him? Hell. Right there. Man when you been to your ophthalmologist? Shit. Look right at that bush there. Now look down at the bottom of that bush. Now run your eyes sideways till you see that little tree root right there and you can see his toe. That's what I'm looking at's his toe. You see that little tree root? And you don't see that toe? Bwana, I think I'm fixing to call me up a gunbearer with a little bit of smarts. Look, man. Put your nose right beside my finger and look down it. You don't see him? Bwana, you making me nervous. You supposed to be able to take care of this shit.

Come on, now. Anybody could see him.

Rufus, bring me that damn .458 up here. Gonna have to shoot the son of a bitch myself I reckon. Man. Johnny Weissmuller would roll over in his grave.

Come on, Bwana. All you got to do is aim about seven or eight feet in front of that toe. Candy *ass*. Gimme that damn gun. Go set your ass down over there on one of them damn anthills. Sheeit.

Don't know what I was doing that shit for. Couldn't stand to hear him talk about that girl no more, I guess. I knew he was gonna wind up telling me they legged down. That stuff hard to take. And it wasn't much time left anyway. I know how long a night is. Laid through enough of them. Wide awake. You sleep all day, you sleep enough, it do something to you. Don't want to sleep then. And no place to run to but a place in your head.

I know it would have been fine over there. Make you a little house out of sticks and don't have no light bill, catch fish in the river, hunt for your food. That old sun looking about ten miles wide going down over the plains. And maybe be just standing out there with your spear in the late evening watching it go down.

You'd be so happy. So happy in your own place.

Something came over him, and I could tell that he'd left me. He turned his head away but he didn't close his eyes. I knew he was tired. And if he didn't want me to talk, I didn't want to. I had my own thoughts. I couldn't do anything for him. I wished there was something I could do for him, but there was nothing. There was too much in my head. The dope had started that. I could have talked non-stop to him, but he wasn't listening anymore. The whole thing was depressing the shit out of me anyway. I didn't want to be on a downer. I felt like I was starting to come out of a long dry spell where there had been nothing but that, and I didn't want to go back to it. All I had to do was get back home, and everything would be all right. I knew that.

I kept looking at him, but he wouldn't look at me. He was looking at something else. I don't think he was even seeing the place he was in. Not right then.

I felt bad. I was pretty sure I was going home in the morning, and he was staying right where he was. For who knew how long? I could see him as an old man, with gray in his hair. And then I said, no, it couldn't be. It wouldn't be right. I thought about what he had been leading up to earlier. And his voice, when it came, came in a whisper, but one in which I could hear every word.

"What if a horse broke its leg? You'd shoot it, wouldn't you?"

I shook my head. "I might not. I might carry it to the goddamn vet if it was a good horse."

I could tell that pissed him off. "All right, then. A old broke-down horse thirty year old, blind, lame, not no good for nothing."

"Don't start," I said. "Don't start on that again. I'm gonna drink a couple more beers and wait on my mama to call. Then I'm gonna tell her to send my brother up here after me. And if you want to talk, we'll talk. But not about that." I looked at him. "It's murder anyway."

"It *ain't*."

"Look, man, it's murder. Any way you look at it. I've seen all that shit on TV. The law sees it as murder."

"I seen that shit on TV, too. I seen that shit on that TV till I'm sick of it. Law ain't in here anyway. Ain't nobody gonna see you. What, you think somebody gonna see you?"

I took a deep breath and looked at the ceiling. He made me feel so fucking guilty. "I ain't doing it. Find somebody else. Cause I don't want to hear no more of it. Nothing else. Crazy motherfucker. I ain't it."

"Yeah you is," he said. "I done been told. You it. I done had me a vision. Jesus done come to see me."

"What?" I said. "Jesus? You been talking to Jesus?"

"Damn right."

Now I know you can talk to Jesus. You can talk to Him all day long. But I've always sort of figured it would be kind of hard to get Him to answer back.

"That must be nice," I said.

"It is."

"Talk to Him regular, do you?"

"When I get ready to."

"What do you talk about?"

"Different stuff."

"You ever talk about murder any? What does He think about murder? Did you ask Him about that? About murder?"

He took his time before he answered. "He knows what murder is. He was murdered Himself. He done been through a murder. He knows about suffering. He done been through that, too."

"What does He say about you?"

"That I ain't gone be here much longer."

"You talked to Him about me?"

"A little."

"What does He say about me?"

"You wasn't the main subject we was talking about. Your name just come up in conversation. So don't get the big head. We wasn't mainly talking about you. We was mainly talking about me. You ain't the one He come to see anyway. I'm the one He come to see."

"Did you ask Him about murder, though?"

He was quiet for a long time. But finally, he said, "Yeah."

"And what did He say?"

"He said I was treading on shaky ground."

I leaned back and got a sip of my beer. "All right, then. There's your answer. Jesus don't condone that kind of stuff. Hell, Braiden. You know that."

"This is different, though."

"How? How's it different?"

He turned and looked at me. "You pissing me off, man, you know that? Why you got to piss me off? Why don't you just listen?"

"I've been listening all night."

"Naw you ain't. You been mostly talking. And when you wasn't talking you wasn't listening. Cause you ain't heard a damn thing I been saying."

I started to laugh. But something inside me said, *No, don't do that. If you do that, you won't hear what he's wanting to tell you.*

"Then tell me," I said.

"All right. I will. First thing you got to realize is people can have things happen to them that ain't their fault. Ain't their fault but they got to pay for it anyway. You got a man out here goes and buys him a bottle of whiskey and gets out on the road drinking it and gets drunk. Now while this man doing this, this lady's got her kids in the car bringing them home from the zoo or somewhere. They ain't even touched a drop. Don't even drink. They ain't done nothing wrong. Go to church every Sunday. And this dude over here, he just getting drunker and drunker while they looking at the lions and stuff. Maybe he got some kind of problem, woman done left him or something, don't matter. Maybe he ain't got nothing wrong. Maybe he just wanting to get drunk cause he like to. All right. He runs head on into them cutting seventy miles an hour. Breaks his neck. Kills all the kids and cuts the lady's legs off. Paralyzes him for the rest of his life. She in a wheelchair for the rest of her life and all her younguns dead. Who's in the worst shape? She'd knowed that motherfucker was coming, she'da stayed home. Or took a different road. And you know he wishing for the rest of his life that he'd either not bought that whiskey or if he did buy it drink it at home or if he was gonna kill somebody then just drive his car into a big oak tree and kill himself and not fuck nobody else up. But it too late then. He got to live with it. The lady got to live with it. One little mistake. Being in the wrong place at the wrong time. If she'da missed one red light it wouldn't've happened. You see what I'm saying? There is things you ain't got no control over. And everybody want to blame it on God. Or say God done it. Say Oh God made that happen. It's for the best. He got a plan in the scheme of everything. I've heard preachers get up and tell it. Stand up in church and say it. Listen, Walter. God don't cause no shit like that to happen. You think He'd let some kid burn up in a house? When He could pick that house up and blow the fire away? He does it sometimes. They showed on TV other night a baby fell off a balcony in a hotel in Georgia, seventeen stories. A little old bitty baby. Now that baby was dead, by all rights, soon as he fell off. But naw. He hits in a palm tree, one hundred seventy feet down, bruises him up a little, falls down through the limbs, and lands in some nice soft grass. Now what does that say to the parents of that baby who wasn't watching him when he crawled out on that balcony? That say The Lord watching you. That say Now I done give you back this baby that you shoulda lost. But I ain't gonna do it again. It say I cain't stop every bad thing that happens all over the world, cause that's y'all. But I stepped in this one time for you. And don't you forget it.

"Now what you think them parents gonna be like with that baby from now on? Shit. They ain't gonna let it out of their sight. When it gets sixteen or seventeen years old they'll be trying to think of some excuse to make him stay at home. Cause they done seen *what coulda been.*

"But He cain't protect everybody. And bad things happen every day. Hundreds of times a day. Thousands of times a day. The thing that happened to me that day was just one thing that happened in the middle of a lot of bad things that happened that day. Shit, Walter. It was over three hundred killed some weeks. He ain't responsible for all that. It ain't no way. Man does all this stuff to himself.

"But listen here. Innocent people always going to be killed. Children going to be killed in war. Ain't no worse crime than that. But you've seen it, ain't you? You know what it was like. Booby-trap anything they could lay their hands on. Pack of cigarettes. Can of beer. Piece of trash. And they was taught. Politicians get up on TV and talk about how bad war is. Don't nobody have to tell people.

People shooting other people is bad and don't nobody have to tell you, you born knowing that.

"What I'm saying is, now listen to me. I have done *paid* my price. I was unlucky and black and young and poor and they drafted me. But I believed in the American dream. Serve your country, do your part, come on home and take a active part in society. You know what I was gonna be? A schoolteacher. Yeah. I was gonna get me a college education, man, on the GI Bill, go to college. Woulda made my mama so happy. I was gonna build her a little house cause she ain't never had one. Nothing but damn shacks. Have to patch the windows up with plastic. I was gonna take all them little black kids and teach em how to read and get em a job and a chance to break loose. Man, you don't know what it was like. To be so damn poor. And have to live on welfare.

"Shit. Listen to me raving. Naw, man, I was raving. It just pisses me off the way everything is. It don't have to be like this. What would this country be like, man, if they never had brought none of us over here? But that's history. You can't change it. Just like this. Just like you. You can't change what happened to you. But there ain't nothing else I can do in this world, Walter. I can't help it. My chance was gone twenty-two years ago. I ain't doing nothing but waiting to die. I don't want to get into it no deeper. I done spent enough time thinking about it. I know my life been wasted, but they's a bunch of good men's lives been wasted. Fifty-eight thousand and something for good. I don't know how many more. Like me. Stuck in places like this. I'm sorry, man. I have to cry. I have to cry for all them wasted lives, man, all them boys I loaded up just like they loaded me up. I couldn't believe it, man. I couldn't believe it had happened to me. I laid on my back and I said it loud. I said Oh Lord, they have shot me all to pieces."

I wanted another beer, but no more grass. I wanted to tell him the rest of it without being messed up. I judged daylight to be about an hour away. So there wasn't a whole lot of time.

I didn't want to think about him when I walked out the door. I didn't want to look back at him just lying there, watching me leave. I wanted to go home and watch my movies and read my books and never see or talk to anybody like him again because he was the thing I had lived through, the thing that marched through my nightmares every night. Young and black and poor. 4-F, you lucky fuckers, you flatfooted fuckers with your high blood pressure. Blind sumbitches, can't even see the damn rifle sights.

Sir! My first General Order is! To take charge of this post and all government property in view! Stick it out if you want it, prives. Take everything you want but eat everything you take. Except for you fatbodies. You fatbodies all you get is salad. TWENTY THIRTY EIGHT! MARCHING IN TO CHOW! AYE AYE SIR! GANGWAY!

Port side make a headcall.

PORTSIDEMAKEAHEADCALLSIR!

Starboard side make a headcall.

STARBOARDSIDEMAKEAHEADCALLSIR!

Damn. Y'all don't want to shit today, do you? I can't even hear you. Port side make a headcall.

PORTSIDEMAKEAHEADCALLSIR!

Listen up. If you slimeball scuzbags of piss-complected puke want to shit today, you better do some screaming. I want you to scream until this squadbay rattles. I want you to scream until your lungs rupture. I was thinking about letting the smokers scream for a cigarette, but if you motherfuckers can't scream any louder than that for a shit, we might just do some bends and thrusts. Many many of them motherfuckers. Starboard side make a headcall.

STARBOARDSIDEMAKEAHEADCALLSIR!!!!

Move.

Then the sumbitch would walk up and down for a while in his boots in front of us, the ones who'd risked not going to the head until nightfall in hopes of getting a cigarette, the ones who hadn't rushed madly into the head, knowing that he might call Clear The Head just as soon as they got their pants down, the ones who were still locked up tight in front of their footlockers, just waiting for that ten-second chance to spring to the combination lock, get it right in absolutely only one try, withdraw one cigarette and a book of matches, shut the lid, snap the lock, and be back at attention in front of the rack, every one, every one in ten seconds. At attention.

Smokers draw one.

SMOKERS DRAW ONE, AYE AYE, SIR!

Shit. You people don't want a cigarette. You people want to do some bends and thrusts. You people should have went in there and took a shit while you had the chance. Clear the head.

CLEAR THE HEAD, AYE AYE, SIR! TEN! NINE! EIGHT! SEVEN! (They'd be running out by then, pulling their pants up, hopping, trying to make it back to their bunks.) SIXFIVEFOURTHREETWOONE!

Freeze!

You had to stop where you were when he hollered freeze. And you had to freeze. In whatever position you were in.

Smokers make a headcall. I mean smokers draw one.

SMOKERS DRAW ONE, AYE AYE, SIR!

Move.

If everybody made it, then we had to get the bucket. The bucket man took care of that.

Smokers outside on the grass across Panama Street.

SMOKERS OUTSIDE ON THE GRASS ACROSS PANAMA STREET, AYE AYE, SIR!

Move.

We'd fly in a herd down the outside stairs, tripping, falling, holding onto that one cigarette, in a mad rush to get across there and formed in a circle before he changed his mind. In a circle at attention with the bucket man in the center. We wouldn't look, but we'd know he was standing on the landing at the top of the stairs across Panama Street, watching us. We'd be hearing the ones who hadn't made it out of the head on time doing their bends and thrusts. Many many of them motherfuckers. But we wouldn't laugh. We wouldn't do anything until he called, real softly:

Let's hear it.

SIR! EVEN THOUGH THE SURGEON GENERAL! HAS DETERMINED! THAT CIGARETTE SMOKING IS HAZARDOUS TO YOUR HEALTH! WE REQUEST PERMISSION TO SMOKE ANYWAY!

And if he liked what he'd heard, he'd call again, real soft:

Light em up.

We all marched in the street. We'd been there a little over a week and the smoking lamp was lit. We were standing out there in a smoking circle and we heard this noise coming down the street. Something steady, regular, hard, stomping the street. Some kind of a disciplined herd of animals, it sounded like, and it was getting closer. Whop whop whop whop. Like stormtroopers, like something with incredible purpose that only death could turn aside.

He called to us. You hear that? You know what that is coming down the street? It's a platoon of U.S. Marines. Thirty seventy, they're graduating tomorrow. You hear that? Snap. Pop. Go ahead and look.

We looked. Forty third-phase recruits were putting two feet down together. Their black DI was singing cadence to them. The flag on their guidon was snapping in the breeze.

You hear that? They'll charge a machine-gun nest right now and not even think about it. Cause they've got discipline. Cause they love my Marine Corps. Tarawa. Okinawa. Iwo Jima. Tripoli. They'd rip your guts out and eat em if he told em to.

He stopped while they passed. The noise they made with their feet covered us. Their boots were spit-shined. Their legs moved like one leg. The precision of the noise was enormous and it came beside us and went by and then it started to fade as they went on down the street. But it was something you could hear for a long way if you listened. We did. We listened until it was gone, until they were gone.

We got an image to uphold here. The best in the world. There's a bunch of them going over there in a few months that ain't coming back. They're gonna die for their country, they're gonna die for their Marine Corps, for all the softass civilians like you guys used to be. The war ain't getting better. It's getting worse. Now you pay afuckin tention or your ass comes home in a plastic bag. Don't die for your country! Make that motherfucker die for his! Do you understand me?

And we roared when we answered him.

Well, I'd done almost lost my faith. He was dead set against it and didn't even want to hear it. He was just laying there, he wasn't doing nothing. Looking at the ceiling. Thinking about his woman, I guess. About them legging down. I don't know. I started talking to him. Told him I knew he thought I was crazy and everything but it was just that he was just now seeing what it was like. He left the war, he come home and tried to forget it. Which every man do. It ain't nothing you want to dwell on. Just something you got to do and then try to forget it. Some can, some can't. Wind up like this, they ain't no way to ever forget it. And he didn't say nothing, he just listened.

Wasn't no way he could ever forget it either. Knew that. But I tried to make him see what a long time it had been. How many days and nights. Told him about how they first had me in Bethesda, how young I was. When my mama first come to see me for the first time.

She didn't know nothing about riding no plane. Never had been on one in her life. Probably scared her almost to death to have to do that, drive up to Memphis and get on a big plane with a bunch of strange people and leave the ground for the first time.

I didn't want her coming. Didn't want her to see me like this. Knew she was going to have to eventually. Tried to put it off long as I could. But the government made all the arrangements. Took care of all that shit. They told me she was coming. And wasn't no way I could run. One morning I woke up and she was standing there looking at me. Holding her purse. My mama.

She said How you doing, son? Voice just shaking. Didn't know I'd lost my arms and legs. Somebody fucked up the paperwork. She was trying not to cry. Just standing there holding her purse. People walking all around us not paying attention. Which the ward was full of guys like me. Some worse, some not as bad. Some just missing only one leg or one arm. Lucky ones. Could still get around, get a job, make out. Go on with their lives. That was when I first started wishing I was dead. It woulda been a lot better for her to see me in my coffin laid out and watch them put me in the ground and blow taps over me than to see me like that. Cause she could have accepted that. It wouldn't have killed her. This what killed her.

They put her in a hotel room on the base. She come to see me every day. She'd feed me. Do other stuff for me. You know. Took care of me for about two weeks. But you could see her going down every day. Never knew my daddy. He run off a long time ago. All my brothers up in Michigan. Work in them car factories up there. They all older than me. Never did know some of them too well. They took off early too. Mama said they was like my daddy, never could stay in one place long. Said he stayed in Mississippi longer than anywhere.

Aw a few of em been to see me a few times. They uneasy when they come, though. We try to talk and it like, you know, they got eyes for everything else but me. Hell, they getting pretty old now, some of em. Got grandchildren, some of em. You can't blame em. Be a relief to them if I was dead, I told Walter. Then they wouldn't have to think about me and feel guilty for not coming to see me too much. Just go on and bury me and come down here one last time and get it over with. Cause they ain't none of em gonna come back down here and live. They got their own lives up there. They don't need to have to feel guilty over me.

He never said nothing. Just laid there and listened to me. I told him how she went on back after about two weeks, cause I had to stay. She'd left my little sister down there with some folks. Had to get on back and see about her. I think she was in like the third grade. And my mama was already old. She was old when she had me. I never saw my daddy. If you want to know the truth I don't think my daddy was my daddy. Couldn't have been. Been gone too long. Know he wasn't my little sister's daddy. Cause he never did come back.

Hell, we growed up with the blues. I know them places in Clarksdale. Them hot summer nights. Streets full of people walking, music playing. Blues was all we had. That and a damn hoe handle.

He never did say nothing. Finally I told him to go on talking. He was leaving in the morning, I wanted to hear what he had to say.

Took him a long time to open back up. I don't know what was going through his mind. I wasn't through with him. There was still plenty of beer left. And I wanted him to keep on drinking it. Keep on drinking it. Keep on drinking it.

"Aw, shit. I don't know, man. I hate to keep bending your ear. But I just can't figure out what the hell happened. You don't know what I felt like waking up in this place. It scared the shit out of me.

"You want anything? You sure? Well. It's been a long night, hasn't it? The most I've talked in a long time. Or the most I guess since I talked to her that night. What was the last thing I told you? I told you about the dog, and about her daddy. I didn't tell you about us going down to the creek, did I? I don't think I told you about that.

"Well. The damn mosquitoes got bad all of a sudden. Started eating us up. We tried covering up with the quilt but you could hear them little sumbitches zmmm zmmm in there with us. So I said Hell let's just go somewhere else. Go get in the car and go ride around or something. I told you about Moore Creek, didn't I? And see, hell, it hadn't rained in I don't know how long. I know you've heard about the drought this year. People around home were cutting hay one week and having to feed it to their cows the next week. A bunch of farmers lost their ass. They even stopped them from irrigating down in the Delta. So hell, Moore Creek was dry. But even when it's not dry there's a place you can pull off in down there because they did away with the bridge. It's not far from the house. But we went by the house first, just to look. And the light was on in my room. And I knew I'd turned it off when we left. What it was, Max was in there. Max. Hell yeah. See, I figured if everybody was asleep at my house, we'd just go back to my room. We could've watched a movie and turned the air conditioner on and just, you know, been more comfortable. But he was in there. If he thinks I'm gone and gonna be gone for a while, he'll go in there and watch a movie. I've got a bunch of good ones. Hell, he may be smoking my dope, I don't know. I think a lot of times he just looks at stuff in my room. Those *Life* pictures and stuff. I've got some other shit hanging up in there. I've got a big piece of exploded shrapnel that's just jagged all over, razor-sharp edges. This colonel who was a friend of mine got it home for me. Colonel Bill. We called him the Supreme Chicken.

"Anyway. I don't mean to digress so much. It's hard

to get to talking about one thing without talking about another thing. But my brother was in my room. So we couldn't go in there. But she wanted to know what he was doing in there. We were pulled up out on the road in front of my house. So I said Hell, let's just go see what he's up to. I didn't mean to do it. But I was fucked up. Hell, I'm fucked up right now. I wouldn't be talking all this shit if I wasn't. But anyway the next thing I knew I had her by the hand and I was leading her across the yard. It was thundering. A bunch of big old black clouds had rolled up. Lightning was flashing way off. We just eased up to the window. The light was on inside, so I knew he couldn't see us out there. I just wanted to see what he was doing. I didn't care for him being in my room. Hell, he's my little brother, I love him. He didn't ask for everything to be the way it is.

"This is my brother, now. Cuts pulpwood for a living. Loves to fight better than he loves to eat. Inherited that shit from Daddy, I guess. He was laid up in my Barco-Lounger with a joint in one hand and a Budweiser in the other, watching *Easy Rider*. I mean he was laid *back*. We just stood there for a minute and watched him. We could see the TV. We didn't mess with him. We just watched him for a little bit. He was into it, man, I could tell. But I was so glad to be with her. I was so damn happy standing out there with her, holding her hand, looking in at Max. I wanted to take care of her. Protect her. I had all these feelings that I'd wanted to have for so long.

"I mean, I used to hear guys talk all the time. Oh hell,

I fucked so and so. I could never understand how they could tell that shit. I mean, if a girl is going to share something that intimate with you, it'd take an asshole to go out and tell the whole world about it. I whipped a guy bad over that shit one time. There was a girl who used to go to school with us, her name was Mary Barry. Don't laugh, now. She had great big titties and great big glasses. Like Coke bottles. She couldn't even hardly see her way around. I mean she had a bad eye problem. Damn, man. This is going way back. Do you want to hear this shit? All right. Well, Mary, now, she was sweet. Had them big humongus jugs. Couldn't see a thing. Everybody'd help her with her papers and stuff. I used to help her. I was trying to help her on a biology test one day and the teacher said I was cheating on the son of a bitch and gave me a zero. So Mary felt bad, you know, because I got a zero from trying to help her. And she was like smart as hell, she just couldn't see anything. And there was this bastard named Charles Chilton who started to school with us in the second semester of the tenth grade. His daddy was the plant supervisor at the factory. And most everybody else's daddy worked at the plant. So he thought he was the supervisor of the school, too. There was a bunch of people wanted to whip his ass, it wasn't just me. He had all these button-down collars and penny loafers and shit. He had a car. Hell, didn't none of us have a car. We'd just have to hitch a ride. But that bastard started messing around with Mary Barry. I mean, she was kind of plain, you know? But she had this great body. And I think she'd had a hard life, she'd been through a divorce with her mama and daddy, and she was sweet. Hell. She used to come over to our house and study with me. Before that bastard got there.

"Damn. Grade school stuff. High school stuff. You lose all these people.

"He had a car, see. A brand new Mustang. He could pick up anybody he wanted to. This was in 1965 or some shit, way back there. Well. We were all down at the Kream Kup one night and saw Mary with this guy. And she was just latching onto him, man, oh it hurt me. I wanted to just kill his ass right there. But I guess you're scared of money and power at first. Everybody hated his ass. We watched them when they left out. I stood out there for I don't know how long, man, just thinking about Mary. About how that son of a bitch was probably going to take her off somewhere and fuck her.

"And that's what he did. Took her off out in the woods somewhere and fucked her. Monday morning he was telling everybody about it. Aw yeah. He told it so much it got back to Mary. I mean her friends were asking her, Did you really do that with him? Something like that, back then, for us, was big time. That was almost unbelievable. People we knew actually fucking. We just couldn't hardly get over it.

"Yeah. He had to spread it all over the whole school. What he'd done to Mary. I heard the first little rumor of it and it made me sick to my stomach. And I saw her going down the hall, crying, bent over, like she was toting some weight. She knew everybody was talking about her. I tried to talk to her and she wouldn't talk. And I knew then that it was actually true, that he'd actually fucked her. I just couldn't hardly believe it. Sweet little Mary Barry? Had actually opened her legs and let somebody put his dick in her? And of all people, that creep? It just liked to killed me.

"He was blowing his shit in the lunchroom about two days later, about how he'd fucked her. And I guess I just went crazy. I was sitting right across the table from him. And he started talking about all the pussy he'd been getting lately. I remember what he had on his plate. Mashed potatoes and peas, and fried chicken. Son of a bitch. I pushed his face right down in those peas and mashed potatoes. Bastard knew better than to talk about her like that. And he thought he was gonna box when he got up. Had those mashed potatoes and peas all over his face. I just totally detested the son of a bitch. Because of Mary. What he'd done to her. God, she was so sweet.

"They finally had to pull me off of him. They liked to kicked me out of school over it. That was two years before I enlisted, I think.

"There's some sorry motherfuckers in the world, Braiden. They're just laying out there waiting. I ain't no angel myself. But damn I don't know why people don't know how to act. I'm too much of a hothead anyway. I've always been bad about doing something before I thought about it.

"But I didn't get mad at Max for being in my room. Hell, it was okay. I knew he had a lot of stuff on his mind and didn't know what to do. I mean about Mama and all. So we just left him in there. He never even knew we'd been there. We just left. Went riding around.

"I started telling her about my mother and my brother, about how I couldn't talk to them. I know they can't stand the way I am, but they act like it's worse on them than it is on me. Hell, that's crazy. I mean, how do they think *I* feel? I'm the one that's got to wear it around. That's the main reason I started just staying in my room. They wanted me to go back to the hospital and have some more work done on my face. What they really wanted was for me to have that operation. But the doctors never could decide what they wanted to do. And I didn't want to do it anyway. I never wanted to be in a hospital again. I know in a way I'm lucky. At least I can still see and hear, I've got my legs and arms, I can walk and talk and get around. You'd swap places with me, wouldn't you? Right.

"They didn't know what to say when they first saw me. I don't know but that it might have been harder on Daddy than anybody. He knew there wasn't anything he could say that would make me feel better. So he didn't say anything. He just started drinking worse. And he was already drinking bad enough. I was no teetotaler either. But we never drank together. We never swapped any war stories. You'd think we would have, but we didn't. Most of the stuff I heard him tell was long ago. He didn't want to talk about his shit, and I didn't want to talk about mine. I never even saw the guys I was with the day I got hit again. I wrote letters to some of them. There was one black guy I knew from Detroit. Tommy Joiner. Little bitty guy. Could box like a motherfucker. He'd been boxing all his life and got drafted. Don't think the marines can't draft you. They can. In wartime they can. He was out of the Kronk gym, where Hearns came from. And all he thought about was getting out and turning pro. He'd won over sixty amateur bouts, a lightweight. They put a little more weight on him at Parris Island. I think he could have made it as a pro. He had a hell of a left hook. And fast, God he was fast. I remember the first time I saw him. He was straight, now, he was all God and country. Tried to keep his brass shined and his boots clean. He was standing in line in front of me one day, one morning, they were frying eggs for us. We hadn't had a fried egg in a while. This guy behind him was telling him to hurry up, hurry up, like Tommy was holding the line up. Hell, Tommy was just waiting on his eggs like everybody else. We had our little mess kits and everything. This sumbitch kept on talking his shit. And the cooks were going as fast as they could, had about fifty eggs going at one time. They were hollering out what did you want, sunny-side-up or over-easy or what. Tommy hollered out he wanted him three over-easy. This guy told him to hurry up again, he was holding the whole line up. Old Tommy just turned around and looked at him. But the guy just kept on. Finally he said something about god-damn choicey niggers. Tommy didn't even know me. He just leaned around the guy and said, How about holding this for me? Handed me his mess kit and his fork. He hit that son of a bitch and dropped him like he was shot. I stepped out of the way and let him fall. He knocked over about three tables, a bunch of hash browns fell on the ground and all. Anyway they busted Tommy down to private because the guy he hit was a corporal. He was just a PFC. And he wouldn't start any shit with anybody. He could damn sure finish it, though.

"He was the one they usually sent down in the tunnels. I was lucky. I was too big to get down in them. Whenever we'd find one, we'd stop and they'd get Tommy to go down. The lieutenant would let him have his pistol. Most of the time there was nobody home. But they'd leave little greetings and stuff for whoever went down. They'd wire a grenade to go off in your face or something like that. Or if they were going to leave it, dig a punji pit and cover it up. Shit on them sticks. It gave me nightmares thinking about going down in one. He wasn't scared, though. He wouldn't say anything about it. He'd just strip off his gear and take the forty-five and head on down. Lots of days nothing happened. You couldn't ever tell where the other openings were for sure and you had to watch in case somebody popped up shooting. Just like that one you were talking about. Some would come up in a hootch, some would be out in the edge of a field. Some days we'd hear that forty-five pop down there in the ground. Tommy'd finally come up and the lieutenant would say, Anybody home? Tommy'd just grin. Give him his pistol back. They was home but they wasn't expecting company, he'd say.

"I was telling her all this stuff while we were riding around. We were drinking beer. It was nice. But she asked me whatever happened to Tommy and I had to tell her. He got killed in a tunnel, finally. That's what I heard back when I wrote. A guy named Miller answered my letter. He said they'd been out on a patrol while I was in the hospital and found a tunnel. They stopped and Tommy went down. And something blew in just a second. They waited a while and let the smoke clear and then sent somebody else in. He'd crawled over a wire just inside the entrance that was rigged to a grenade. They had to gather him up and ship him home to his mama. He's in the picture. Putting me on the helicopter. Tommy.

"You about to go to sleep? Oh. You were so quiet I thought maybe you were asleep. Hell, I'm just talking. Just about drunk.

"I didn't want to bore you. I know I'm talking too much. I talked to Beth for a long time. I told her everything.

"We didn't want to run Max out, he looked like he was having a good time. He has to put up with Mama so much. And she wanted to go park somewhere, so hell, I told her Let's pull off down in Moore Creek. So we got back in the car and drove down there, pulled off in there and stopped. It was dark as hell. Just barely could see her next to me. We kissed a little was all. Nothing heavy. We were still talking. Hell, I figured we had all night.

"She wanted to know some more about my daddy. And I didn't know how much to tell her. He was the kind of person who wouldn't take any shit off anybody. I mean none. If you said something smart to him you'd better be ready to whip his ass or have yours whipped one. Cause that's all there was to it. If you popped off to him you were fixing to fight. His temper got him into trouble. That and his drinking.

"See, he killed a guy when I was little. And he stayed in the pen five or six years for that. And he was on probation for several years after that. He didn't have enough money to start back farming full time. He'd just get little jobs wherever he could. People don't forget it when you kill somebody. So things were kind of rough for us. I mean one thing just leads to another. We were poor as hell, man, I'm not lying to you. We had to work at whatever we could. And one thing he was good at was picking cotton. He'd been picking it all his life. They picked it every year down at Parchman. He was one of the top field hands down there. And he'd hire out every fall to pick for folks around home. That was one job he could get because he was so fast.

"So we were working for this man one year. Daddy'd been out of the pen for a few years, I guess. And I could pick a pretty good bit myself so I went with him.

"There'd been a few times when he'd been in jail for fighting. They'd done told him if he didn't straighten his ass up they were going to send him back to Parchman for a while. And hell, he'd try. Mama would sit him down and talk to him. And he'd go along good for a while. Then he'd get ahold of a little money. He'd go buy groceries and then he'd buy a bottle with what was left. Then the law would drive out to the house and tell Mama they had him in jail again. That was the way things were going then.

"This guy we were working for, Daddy didn't much like him. I don't know what there was between them. It rubbed him the wrong way to have to work for him, but we needed the money so he went on and did it. And you just didn't see many white people picking cotton. Most of them were black. People moved around then, picked cotton wherever they needed them.

"So we were working for this guy. His name was Norris. I guess he was about the same age as Daddy. Maybe a little older. He's dead now. Turned a tractor over on him snaking logs out a couple of years ago. He's the one who got Daddy sent back to the pen.

"We had a crew come in there one day, a whole family, had sideplanks on their truck and all their stuff in there, little black kids all piled up in the back. There were some other people in the field, too, but it was about thirty acres. With a picker now that's nothing. But back then most of it was picked by hand.

"Anyway they drove up and asked old Norris if he needed any help. He said he did and the guy asked him what he was paying. So Norris told him and asked him reckon when they could start. This guy says Wellsuh we figgered we'd start in right now. So, hell, they all piled out, it was seven or eight of them, some little bitty kids, too. Cutest little kids. Some of them had their hair fixed up like Buckwheat when he was little, you know. That guy I guess was in his early forties, middle forties. His wife got out and helped. Every one of them helped except for a little baby they had. They let it sleep in the truck.

And they started in around two o'clock that evening. That guy's name was Louis Champion. He got on a row beside Daddy and they went to picking some cotton. Daddy was pretty good, but this guy could pick more, and cleaner, than anybody I ever saw. He didn't pull any trash and he didn't leave anything behind, either. They even had their own sacks. It was what they did every fall. They went wherever there was cotton, didn't matter where it was.

"Wasn't but about an hour before Champion came out with his sack full and laid it down and got another one, squatted down and smoked a cigarette, and then hit it again. Hell, Norris knew how hard he was working. Daddy came over to me one time and said Damn, that guy beats anything I've ever seen. Said he couldn't keep up with him. He had a fourteen-year-old girl who could pick almost as much as Daddy could. I guess they'd done it all their lives. Or maybe there wasn't much other way for them to make money the other parts of the year, and they had to make all they could in a season. Anyway they worked harder than any people I've ever seen. Him and Daddy talked just about all evening, I mean when they could. Champion had been in the war, too. I guess they were talking about that.

"Long about dark they were still picking, and Norris hollered out That's enough, let's quit for the day. And hell, I was ready to. Most times we'd get paid by the day. You got paid when the sun went down. But we still had a bunch to pick. And I don't know what all was said exactly but it turned out they didn't have any money for supper and wanted to spend the night and just stay till it was all picked. Till the whole field was picked. And which that suited old Norris fine, he wanted to get it out and get it to the gin before it rained. Go on and get it baled. Get his money.

"So he told em yeah, they could stay on the place. Champion wanted his money for that day, though. Me and Daddy were going to wait on ours. We were going to stay till it was all picked anyway. Norris was writing it down every time we weighed our sacks. We didn't know he was weighing us light. Maybe Daddy knew. Maybe that was why he didn't like to work for him. I don't know. But anyway they stood around talking for a while and Norris talked Champion into just waiting till they got through before he paid him out. Told him he'd give him whatever he needed by the day. Acted real nice about it, of course. He pulled out thirty dollars and gave it to him and said, Just go on and take this, get whatever you need, I'll take it out of whatever I owe you when we get through. Hell, his eyes lit up when he saw that money. He'd probably never been given any advance money his whole life. Norris was watching them weigh the sacks when they brought them out, but this is how he fucked him. How he fucked all of us. He had the cotton scale shaved down to where it didn't show what it ought to. He had some regular scales and then he had these. You couldn't tell it if you didn't know what to look for. He'd milled the damn thing down some way to where it took more weight to bring it down to where it ought to read. Then, I don't know, I guess he left it laying out in the pasture for about a year so it would rust and look like it had always been like that. The first evening they worked, old Champion looked at that scale a little funny. Norris showed him what he had written down in his little book and he kind of turned his head up on the side and said, Sure thought I picked more'n that. Then Norris gave him that money. So, hell, everything was slick. Right then, anyway.

"Daddy told him where the store was and then we left. Our house was just down the road a little ways. They had them a little tent they were setting up when we took off. I thought it was pretty neat. They just lived sort of a nomadic lifestyle, I guess. They had that tent and pots and pans and all. A big Dutch oven, lanterns. Had some cots and a bunch of quilts. They'd just camp out wherever they were working.

"So we went on to the house and ate supper. Mama had fixed a big blackberry pie in a dishpan and there was a bunch of it left over. We were just sitting around the table after supper talking. Mama got up to start washing dishes and she saw those lights down in the field there and asked Daddy what that was. We told her about those people staying down there. Daddy was sitting there smoking a cigarette and he looked at that pie and then looked at me and said, Hell, Walter, let's go down there and carry them kids the rest of that pie. Said they'd probably like some dessert. So we went back down there. Carried some spoons. Tried to get Max to go but he was watching 'Gunsmoke.'

"You should have seen those kids. They all started grinning when they saw that pie. They were all real nice and everything. Champion was sitting in a folding chair smoking a pipe and reading a newspaper when we got there. They had some coffee made and he got us some chairs, fixed me and Daddy some coffee. Had his shoes off. They had a nice little camp there. The kids started eating that pie. Even got that little baby up and fed him some of it. Boy he liked it, too. He was smacking his lips.

"I was raised not to talk when grown people were talking, so I just listened. Him and Daddy talked about the cotton for a while, about what a good crop it looked like. And after a while he said something else about being light on the scales but I didn't know it then, see. It was a long time later when I found out what happened. I went and got the scales one night. While they still had Norris in the hospital and Daddy in jail. I weighed a bag of Portland cement that was certified at ninety-four pounds and the scales said eighty-one. He was cheating us out of about fifteen pounds on every hundred. Which adds up to a hell of a lot on thirty acres. But Champion didn't know for sure. He didn't make any big deal out of it. They got to talking about where all they'd gone in the war. They'd been in a lot of the same places. He had six kids and another one coming. They picked cotton everywhere, all over Mississippi, even went over in north Alabama and picked. They just moved around in the fall, but they lived in Alligator. He said down there they wouldn't pay much for picking, there were so many people needing work, so he'd come up north.

"I don't know. He didn't seem bitter. He knew a better day was coming sometime. He just wished it was here now. Then. He wanted his kids to go to college. Get educations. Not have to pick cotton the rest of their lives. I'd never heard a black man talk like that. I'd never heard one with hopes like that. But finally he yawned once and we got the hint and got up to go. He stood up and his wife brought the pan over, she'd done washed it and all the spoons, and they thanked us for bringing it to the kids. They were good people. They didn't seem like they were unhappy. But I felt sorry for them. Hauling their kids all over the country. Camping out in a tent. I guess it was just the times we lived in. I guess it wasn't just Mississippi. It was the way everything was back then. But you could find people like that right now I know.

"He knew something was wrong by dinnertime the next day. He'd bring his sack out and it would weigh light to him every time. He'd stand there and look at it. He'd picked enough to know what the sack would hold damn near to the pound. Daddy didn't say anything, he was just watching. Maybe Daddy knew Norris was screwing us. Maybe he just wanted to stay out of trouble. But Champion finally said something about it. To Norris. Said I believe it's something wrong with that scale. Well, Norris just flew into cussing. Usually that was all he had to do. Most of them wouldn't stand up to him. But Champion did. I guess Daddy had seen this kind of thing happen before. He didn't say nothing, he just watched. Champion told old Norris he wasn't calling him a cheat, but he knew what his sack would hold. Norris told him if he thought there was something wrong with the scale to go on and look at it, so he did. Hell, it looked all right. You're talking about just a little bit of metal shaved off that made a lot of difference. The whole thing didn't weigh but a few pounds. He looked at it, just shook his head. Said well, it didn't look like they was nothing wrong with it. He just couldn't figure it out. Said I know what my sack holds. Shit, I hated it. It looked like we were fixing to have some real trouble. I didn't know what Daddy was going to do, whether he was going to stay out of it or not. I figured I knew whose side he'd be on. But Champion didn't look like a guy you could push much, either. Only thing was his wife and kids looked scared as hell.

"Finally he went on back in the field and started picking again. Working faster than he was before. He rolled. Worked on through dinner and wouldn't even stop to eat. He was packing it in there. Got it so full it wouldn't hold any more. Just about too heavy to pull. Daddy quit picking and left his sack on the ground and helped him pull it up to the truck. Took both of them to get it up on the hook. I'd never seen one sack with that much in it. Old Norris got up there and fiddled around with it a while and hollered out One twenty-two. And hell, it had over a hundred and fifty pounds in it, easy. And it flew all over Champion. He told him. Said You weighing us short. And hell, everybody could see it. Everybody'd done stopped picking. Old Norris was scared. He eyeballed Daddy a little bit. Then he called Champion a lying black son of a bitch. Right there in front of his wife and kids and everybody. You could tell he really had to suck up his guts to do it. Cause there was Daddy looking at him, too. But Daddy wasn't saying anything. He was just watching.

"Champion said Well, you can just pay us off. Cause we ain't working no more. Norris said that was fine with him. He had it all wrote down. Started figuring it up. Champion got all his kids out of the field and they started packing everything up. Daddy just motioned for me to get out of the field so I did. They had to take down their tent and all. I was trying to figure in my head how much they must have picked. A lot. And if it was fifteen percent he was trying to gyp us out of it was a bunch. Hell. He could've made it right. That's what Daddy was doing, giving him a chance to. Champion was smoking a cigarette, just waiting. Old Norris looked up at him one time and said I doubt if you've made thirty dollars yet, and it was like he'd slapped him. He had this look on his face like the world was fixing to end. Norris put his pencil in his pocket finally and handed Champion the little book he'd been figuring in. He looked at it for a minute. Then he just closed it up and dropped it on the ground. Said I know a ton of cotton when I see it, white man.

"At two cents a pound it would've brought forty dollars. And Norris held out four dollars and told him that was all he was getting. Said that was all he owed him if they didn't pick any more. Champion wouldn't take it. Said You cheating me. Norris started cussing him again. Told him he'd better take it and get off the place. Champion said Why you want to cheat me? Said I ain't never done nothing to you. He said he was taking ten, but he wasn't taking four. Norris throwed the money down. Said there it was if he wanted it, but for them to get their asses gone.

"Daddy was real calm about it. He said If you've cheated this man then you've cheated me too. Me and my boy. But he wasn't even looking at Norris while he was talking. He was looking at Champion's kids. Man, they were scared. They were all holding onto their mama. Daddy said Now you pay him what you owe him and then you pay me.

"Man. I've thought a lot of times how easily all that could have been avoided. All he had to do was be honest. Just wouldn't do it. Just that damn sorry.

"He told Daddy, said Now Randall I ain't got no quarrel with you. Said I'm gonna pay you what I owe you. Daddy said yeah and he was gonna pay them what he owed them, too. Started walking toward him. Norris started backing up. Backing around toward the cab. Champion spoke up and told him to just leave it alone, he could handle it. Didn't need any help. It all happened so fast. If he hadn't been so scared of Daddy it probably wouldn't have happened at all. I mean all this shit happened over six dollars.

"He had the gun under the seat. Little sawed-off twelve-gauge single barrel. It was on the other side of the truck. I didn't actually see it when it went off. Just heard it. I saw Norris fall. We stepped around there and it looked like about half his head was blowed off. There Daddy was holding the gun. Hell, we thought he was dead. So much blood. But he didn't die. Not till he turned that tractor over on him a few years ago. They never did figure out how that happened. He was snaking logs out by himself. Way off down in the woods. Had a fifty-foot cable with a hook on it. Got the damn thing hooked around a tree somehow. That's the thing about a tractor. You don't want to pull nothing with the back end that can't be pulled. They'll turn straight over backward on you. Every time. You'd think a man like that would know to watch behind him. All he lost that day in his cotton patch was one ear and some skin off the side of his head. My daddy lost some more years of his life. And I lost that much more of my daddy. Cause they sent him back to the pen again after that.

"He got me to go call the law and an ambulance and all. He got Champion and them to leave while I was gone. We never heard anything out of them again. Daddy just sat there and waited for the law to come get him. He knew it wouldn't do any good to run. But he gave them the chance to run and they took it.

"He went quick in his sleep one night. Mama woke up next to him and he was already cold. She just laid there beside him and held him until it got daylight. Then she woke us up and told us. But he was old. Looked old, moved like an old man. He did nearly ten years altogether. That's a lot of cottonpicking.

"So Mama calls out to God every night. Praying to die. Because she misses him so much. She just can't get over him being gone. I wish I'd gotten to spend more time with him. I wish I knew why everything has to be the way it is sometimes.

"Anyway I told her all that. It started raining. There wasn't a whole lot to say. We were just holding each other. At first we were. Then we started messing around. Hell, maybe it was sympathy, I don't know. She took her shirt off and got me to take her bra off. It started raining harder and harder. I remember thinking we might ought to back it out of the creek. But I guess we were too busy doing what we were doing. She didn't want me to see her legs. I remember her saying that. About how they were all scarred up. I told her it didn't matter. And it didn't. It was hard to see it in the dark anyhow. And the rain was so nice. We hadn't had any in so long.

"Are you asleep? You want me to hush? I will if you want me to. You sure?

"Well. I've been trying to keep from thinking about it, but that's all I can think about now. Being in that car with her. With the rain coming down. And the doors locked. Knowing nobody was going to interfere with my life this time.

"I mean, it had been so long. I'd been waiting, always thinking something was going to happen. And it never did. I'd hidden from everybody for so long. I just withdrew from the world. Stayed in my room all that time.

She made me feel like somebody again. Instead of just a freak.

"But if you could have seen her. What that dog did to her. God."

He hushed up after that. And I hadn't said a word. Wasn't nothing to say. He finished the rest of his beer and stuck it under his pillow and then he just laid there looking up at the ceiling.

I wasn't sleepy. Wouldn't've been no way to sleep then anyway, after hearing all that. I knew I had to say something else to him. Just didn't know what.

Didn't look like there was no way to fix his troubles. Sure didn't do me no good to hear all that. Wasn't no way I could help him. Couldn't even help my own self. And couldn't ask him to help me but one more time. Cause the night was almost gone. It was time for Diva to be back, but she wasn't. I needed her. I needed her to help me. Cause she knew better than anybody what I been through. She'd done seen me laying here all this time. She knew what had to be done. She just couldn't do it herself. She could do a lot. She'd done done a lot.

But not that. So I was wishing she would hurry. The night was almost gone. And I didn't want to see another one.

I couldn't tell Braiden everything. I couldn't tell him all of it. There was too much that was private. Too much I didn't want anybody to know about her. Because she didn't want even me to see.

Her legs were ripped with scars. And I kissed all those bad places. I told her that it didn't matter. She cried, a little, but I hushed that up. What I was trying to do was soothe her. Make her feel better. It took a long time. I don't know what she was thinking. That I'd run away? Be repulsed? I asked her, How could I?

She told me to kiss her, that she'd been waiting a long time for this. That she'd never had a man, and I was the first. The lightning started. The rain came down harder. That was when the little pain in the top of my head hit me. But those pains are common. They don't always mean something. I've had them for so long that I don't pay much attention to them anymore.

With the grass, everything had slowed down to slow motion. Every movement, every touch of flesh, every breath and every sound. The rain was so loud on the roof, we couldn't hear anything else after a while. It was like a hundred little hammers all beating at once. No other sound. And just as black. We weren't even in the world anymore. There was just us two, and the night.

We were naked together. Me against her. We started trying to ease it in. She put her legs around me. That's the last thing I remember.

I saw a thing I maybe dreamed. It come in the window and lit on my bed and it was a little angel child with gold hair and sandals. It looked at me and smiled and smiled and smiled. It come a crawling over my feet and over my legs and I held out my arms and the child come to rest against my chest. Put its head down against me like it wanted to sleep. I touched the gold hair. The child looked up and smiled and rested with me. We laid there for a long time, just holding on to each other. Don't know how long a time passed. A long, long time. Things that wasn't said flowed from the child to me and I come to understand that he or she was the one they sent to lead me, but it wasn't time to go. And it didn't have to be the time to go. The child could leave, and I could stay, and it would come back for me some other time. But my arms would leave, and my legs would leave, and they wouldn't come back till the child did again.

I touched the hair on the child's head. It was soft and sweet. I held the child. I didn't want to decide. I just wanted to hold the child. But finally it looked at me and I knew it was time to decide. I nodded my head. The child nodded its head. It stood up and walked back across the bed, stepped up on my knee, and stood there balanced, looking back at me. Had its hands clasped together and looking down. It pointed to the foot of the bed. And there He stood.

So you've decided?

Yes, Lord. Won't I be happier there than here?

You're leaving others behind you. What about them?

They'll miss me for a while. One especially. But she'll get over it.

There'll be nieces and nephews later that you won't get to meet. What about that?

If I don't know them then I won't know what I've missed.

Things have been set in motion that you know nothing about. It won't be easy when it comes and you'll wish you hadn't wished for it.

But after that.

Yes, after that.

Will everything be explained to me?

This child will come back.

Will I be whole again?

You're whole now.

Then that's what I want.

It's not what you want. It's going to happen whether you want it or not. I could intercede if you wanted me to. You want me to?

No sir. I don't believe I'd want that.

He held out his arms to the child. The child hopped off my knee and landed in His arms. He stood there holding it on His hip.

For what it's worth you've been brave.

Thank you, Lord.

He sighed.

We'll see you after while.

They left, and I didn't know if any of it was real or not. More than anything I was scared.

I didn't know if Braiden was asleep by then or what. He was quiet, but I was through talking anyway. I'd said all I wanted to say. I was watching the window so I could see when the first of daylight came through it. I wanted to talk to Mama and tell her to send Max after me, and then I wanted to get dressed. I was hoping that maybe he was already on his way.

I saw her coming, just a vague white shape moving toward me out of the darkness. Swishing. I could still hear her stockings. She was still fine.

She sat down on the edge of the bed. One hand swept my hair back and lingered on my jaw.

"Not much time left," she said.

"Time for what?"

"This. Braiden asleep?"

"I don't know. What about my phone call? She called yet?"

She looked around. "In a little bit."

She leaned closer, until she was lying next to me. I could feel her breasts pressing against me. I couldn't move. The smell of her almost drove me crazy and made me think of Beth and made me hate myself. She put her cheek against mine and rested it there.

"Listen to me," she said. "Just listen to me. His mind will go. It's starting to already. He just like you, he ain't gonna get no better."

I closed my eyes, reached out, and put my arms around her.

"I went to nursing school just so I could take care of him," she said. "Ten years. He's the only thing holding me here. I know you in bad shape. Everybody in here in bad shape. Wouldn't be in here if they wasn't. You *might* have a chance. They *might* make you better. They ain't no way they can make him better. He ain't got no chance. He can't lay here till he's sixty or seventy. It ain't right. I started out thinking I could take care of him. Way he used to take care of me. It would of been a mercy if God had let him die when he was supposed to. He ain't got no peace, Walter. He don't want to stay. He wants to go. His life is over."

I said what I knew was a stupid thing: "His life's not over."

She drew back, drew her hands back and put them in

her lap. She sat still, quiet, on the edge of the bed, looking at the floor.

"Put yourself in his place," she said.

I did. I felt my arms and legs still attached to my body. I felt my legs taking me down the road at night, my arm extending to punch the start button on my VCR, my fingers coming up to my lips with a cigarette. I felt Beth in my arms and wished oh God so bad that night could be here again, instead of this.

"You can't just murder people," I said.

She didn't move at first. She didn't seem like she'd even heard me. And then her hand moved to my leg. High.

"Stop fucking around with me," I said.

"You white boys," she said, and a slow easy little laugh came out of her.

Flat on your back for that long. Fed every meal. Rolled over like a sack of shit when it was time to change your sheets. For twenty-two years. I couldn't take it either.

She bent over me then.

"I can take care of it," she said.

"What?"

"You lay back. I take care of you one time anyway," she said. I saw her hand come up, and it was dark against the pale cloth of her uniform. Her hand caught the zipper and pulled it down to her waist. She struggled out of the top of it. She bent her arms behind her back, and took off the bra and laid it aside. She leaned closer, smiling.

"Give you something like you ain't never had, baby," she said.

She started humming the tune, the same one she'd been

humming when she first came to see me. The field song. The picker's song. Her breasts were right over me, just inches away. I thought about Beth. She started pulling her dress up over her hips. Then she was sliding down my belly, raising my gown.

"I do this, and you do that. Cause you don't know what's going on."

It was hard to speak. She had me in her hands. I had to arch my back, and dig my fingers into the sheet.

"He my brother," she said, and then she put her mouth on me, and Braiden started talking to me, and I was drunk, and I knew I was his last chance, but inside I was saying no, please no, hell no, forever no.

"*The Young Lions*. Man you know I had a granma whose daddy was a slave. He was freed and fought at Shiloh, and run at Vicksburg when he seen it was gone, that they was beat. Whole town was starving to death. Had trees, logs stuck up through the bank to make it look like cannons. People was living in caves like rats. Lost his left arm. And he lived to be a hundred and one. You know what he told her?

"Said Jenny, people has been fighting since God made the first one and they always going to. Nothing don't change but the reasons, man. All you can do is love the ones close to you and try to do right. That's all God expects. God can't be blamed for what happens to men. Ain't God's fault what happened to you, to your daddy, or what happened to me. Fifty-eight thousand of ours we lost. Think about it, Walter. Each one thought it wouldn't happen to him. You know how many friends I lost? Seventeen. I mean friends. People I was tight with. Seventeen. I don't have to tell you. I mean you get to know a man, you get to talking to him, he pulls out some pictures sometime and show you. Show you his little girl. His crib. His mama and daddy. He alive to them. They all talking about him at home, wondering when he gonna come back. *Is* he gonna come back. And then he be dead two or three days before they even know it. They don't know you, but you know him, and you the one have to put him in the bag and zip it up. I done that seventeen times.

"World don't change for no man. World gone keep going on. Don't make no difference what you do, what I do. World keep turning. God got a plan for everything. Man may suffer in this world. But God got a better world waiting. I been waiting to see it twenty-two years, Walter. You ain't no man if you don't do this for me. I tired, Walter. I tired and I want to go home. Want to see my mama. She waiting, too.

"You think you got trouble? You don't know what trouble is. Trouble when you laying in a rice paddy knowing both your arms and legs blowed off and are they gonna shoot the chopper down before it can come and get you. Trouble when they pick you up and you ain't three feet long. The people in my fire team started to just let me lay there and bleed to death. Cause they knowed I'd wind up like this if I lived. Knowed I'd lay like this no telling how many years. They ever one of em has come to see me. And they each said the same thing. You know what that was?

"We wish we'd left you, Braiden.

"You been sent to me, Walter. You been sent and I ain't gonna be denied."

It was over, finally. She pulled her clothes back together and left, and Braiden turned his face away. I was weak, and there was nothing else to say. But I knew I wouldn't be back there. All I wanted was to be home.

I waited for daylight a long time and it seemed like it would never come. I wanted the night behind me. I smoked a cigarette, and I made a few decisions.

I wouldn't lock myself away in my room anymore. I'd live with my family and try to help my mother. She was old, and she'd been hurting for a long time, and I didn't want to cause her any more pain. I knew that this thing must have scared her badly, me being out for two days, not knowing what was going to happen to me. I'd try to decide what to do about my face and my head. There were other hospitals and other doctors, and people everywhere ready to help me. I'd take Beth over to the house, and let Mama meet her, and the three of us could talk about it. That was as far as I got.

Diva was standing beside the bed suddenly, saying, in a low voice, "Your mama's on the phone."

I turned my head and looked at her. She wouldn't look at me. She stood with her head down, her hands holding each other in front of her. I got out of the bed, grabbed a robe, and she turned. I put the robe on and I followed her out into the hall.

Nobody was stirring. The nurses' station was deserted. The phone was lying on the counter. Diva sat down, but she wouldn't look at me. She just held her hands folded in her lap. I picked up the phone.

I said, "Mama?"

She was crying. She knew what had happened, and I realized then that Diva knew what had happened. But since I couldn't remember any of it, I had to picture it in my mind, in little flashes of memory before it all went black, how it would have seemed, like somebody watching a movie while she told me.

It was drizzling light rain, rain for the first time in a long time. It was washing the fields. It was cooling the air. He could feel the tiny spots of it landing on his arm.

He told her to pull off into Moore Creek, that nobody could see them from there. She eased the car down into the bottom of it and shut it off. She pushed off the headlights. They sat for a moment, looking at each other. Then they came together.

He helped her take her shirt off. The rain came down on the roof. It was dark in the car; she was kissing him. They were high from the grass. He was messed up and she was messed up and somehow they had found each other like a miracle or dream. And in their combined dreams they were whole, and happy at last, and normal. The rain swelled a little, it lashed at the wheels of the car. He unsnapped her jeans. He could feel the curly hairs just below her waist and he could feel the terrible scars like ridges on leather as he drew her pants off her legs.

I don't want you to see me, she said.

I ain't looking, he said. Just feeling.

Well. That's all right.

He touched her webbed skin and she touched his ruined face.

That dog eat me up.

I know. But I'm going to make everything okay. You're lovely to me. That's all that matters.

It rained harder. For a while it rained harder than he'd ever seen it.

You think we might ought to back the car out of here?

We can back it out if it gets too bad. Not right now. Kiss me. I've been waiting a long time. All night. All my life. Have you slept with a lot of women?

Some.

How many?

I don't know. Hell. I'd have to count them up.

How long's it been since you've slept with one?

A long time.

Since you got hurt?

Since I got hurt.

That's a long time for a man, isn't it?

He smiled at her.

Too long.

The rain murmured and whispered against the windows of the car and he thought of ponchos tented against the rainy nights and the leaves slowly dripping water down on them. He spread her open and she moaned as she took it. He buried his face in her neck. The jungle had been like this, so dark there was no form or shape to it, only the blackness that made your eyes ache. But in the blackness there had been that longing for this, this moment that he was living now. He pushed himself up into her deeper and felt her wrap her legs around him tighter, heard her breath hissing through her slightly parted teeth. Sweet lips and her hair lashed with sweat, struggling against him, like a crippled fish astounded at the shock of dry land. Oh God you're killing me. Do you want me to stop? No. Please don't. I can't. I can't say what I feel. Oh. Please. Yes. Am I hurting you? No. I just. I never thought anybody would want me. I want you. I want you for the rest of my life. The rain and the jungle and the wounded people and the crying babies and the white phosphorous blooms in the air that etched images on the wall of the retina, slow pinwheelings that smoked across the black sky. The red tracers coming every four rounds so slowly you could watch them fly, watch them shatter the brush, watch them seeking you. Jesus, she said, Jesus. I don't mean to hurt you. It's better now. It doesn't hurt as bad. I can take it. Go on. This is just the first time. We've got plenty of other times. I can't wait until the next time. Oh. Damn. Yes.

The rain flowed under the tires and rose over the pattern of logs laid like ties over the low crossing and covered them, rising steadily, the water flowing toward the river. The rain fell over the elms and beeches and water oaks and they trailed it down their trunks and emptied it down their roots and trailing feeder roots, down the gutted banks and over the stones glistening softly in the dark and down the thin shoots of cane into Moore Creek. It rose up under the wheels and covered the axles, bellying up under the frame. It poured down the gravel road and channeled its own escape, washing the gravel with it, seeking lower ground. It thundered, and the lightning snapped, and the car kept rocking gently as the water flowed in over the rocker panels, pooling in the floorboards and rising toward the front seat. She hammered at his shoulder and hammered at his chest and cried out his name, but the weight of him was something dead, something buried deep within her. The water rose onto the seat with her and her hair clung from the back of her head as she tried to keep her nose above it. She called out for God to call back the rain. It slanted down from the high tops of the trees over the car into the creek and foamed up in little shrouds like white lace softly churning and dancing in the muddy water. She pushed his head up and fought his dead weight like something caged or just released and sank back under the ponderous burden of his head and chest and legs. She fought him with everything she had. She tried to draw her legs out and tried to slide him sideways and the water rose over her cheeks, into her ears, into her nose until she strangled and lurched wildly up with it pouring over her head. She took his torn face and with every last ounce of strength she had, pushed it up and over and wedged it into the steering wheel.

A road crew checking bridges and crossings for flash flooding found them, an amazed party slowly advancing with hip boots, their flashlights playing over the water flowing through the car, and coming to rest on the two naked people caught in there like driftwood, his head just inches above the rising water, hers just beneath. He seemed to be sleeping there, on top of her, moving gently in the current.

Going back to the ward with her following me, I thought of images I remembered and hadn't told him. A chopper tilting sideways with black smoke pouring out of it and slamming into a treeline and sixteen men on it all screaming for their mamas as it burst into flames. The picture of my father on the wall of my room, grinning and saluting as he received his Purple Heart. Standing in the middle of a cold and muddy river with the trigger of the M60 locked down and the belt chattering and the drops of water it sprayed up sizzling on the barrel.

And what was he dreaming of when I stood beside his bed? The sleep of all silence, meadows of sheep, green fields of grass? Peace and serenity, or kids like we used to be catching lightning bugs flying. Cotton picking in the Mississippi Delta and the long rows of white and the slow rides back to the barn in the trailers, the wire mesh we used to cling to, the people waving as we passed. I don't think he dreamed of that thing over there. I think he dreamed of Africa, the vast plains his people had come from, the little houses of sticks and the footprints in the dust. The cheetah streaking across the veldt, the lion blinking in the tall brown grass, the elephant, the rhino, the crocodile sliding into the river with one fan of his tail. Impala meat over the coals of a fire and that orange ball of the sun, miles wide, burning down over the horizon while a man with a spear on his shoulder walked in black silhouette across the face of it.

I stood over him for a long moment. He opened his eyes and looked at me when I closed my hands around his throat. He said Jesus loves you. I shut my eyes because I knew better than that shit. I knew that somewhere Jesus wept.

ABOUT THE AUTHOR

LARRY BROWN was born in Oxford, Mississippi, in 1951. He served in the Marine Corps from 1970 to 1972, and in 1973 joined the Oxford Fire Department, where he served as captain until 1990; he now writes full time. Mr. Brown is the author of two short-story collections, *Facing the Music,* which received the Mississippi Institute of Arts and Letters 1989 Award for Literature, and *Big Bad Love*; *Dirty Work* is his first novel. He and his wife, Mary Annie, have three children and currently live in Yocona, Mississippi.

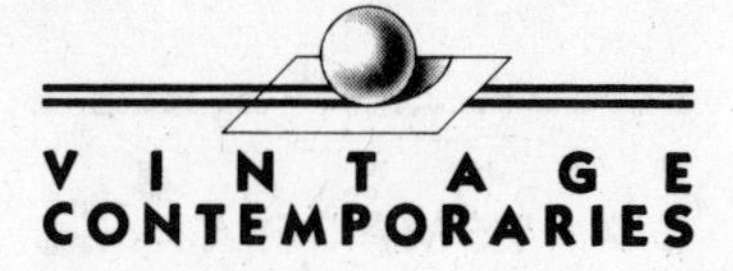

Title	Price	ISBN
I Pass Like Night by Jonathan Ames	\$8.95	0-679-72857-0
The Mezzanine by Nicholson Baker	\$9.00	0-679-72576-8
Room Temperature by Nicholson Baker	\$9.00	0-679-73440-6
Vox by Nicholson Baker	\$8.00	0-679-74211-5
Gorilla, My Love by Toni Cade Bambara	\$9.00	0-679-73898-3
The Salt Eaters by Toni Cade Bambara	\$10.00	0-679-74076-7
Violence by Richard Bausch	\$11.00	0-679-74379-0
Chilly Scenes of Winter by Ann Beattie	\$10.00	0-679-73234-9
Distortions by Ann Beattie	\$9.95	0-679-73235-7
Falling in Place by Ann Beattie	\$11.00	0-679-73192-X
Love Always by Ann Beattie	\$10.00	0-394-74418-7
Picturing Will by Ann Beattie	\$9.95	0-679-73194-6
Secrets and Surprises by Ann Beattie	\$10.00	0-679-73193-8
What Was Mine by Ann Beattie	\$10.00	0-679-73903-3
A Farm Under a Lake by Martha Bergland	\$9.95	0-679-73011-7
The Revolution of Little Girls by Blanche McCrary Boyd	\$10.00	0-679-73812-6
The Planets by James Boylan	\$10.00	0-679-73906-8
Dream of the Wolf by Scott Bradfield	\$11.00	0-679-73638-7
The History of Luminous Motion by Scott Bradfield	\$11.00	0-679-72943-7
A Closed Eye by Anita Brookner	\$11.00	0-679-74340-5
Brief Lives by Anita Brookner	\$11.00	0-679-73733-2
The Debut by Anita Brookner	\$10.00	0-679-72712-4
Fraud by Anita Brookner	\$11.00	0-679-74308-1
Latecomers by Anita Brookner	\$8.95	0-679-72668-3
Lewis Percy by Anita Brookner	\$10.00	0-679-72944-5
Providence by Anita Brookner	\$10.00	0-679-73814-2
Big Bad Love by Larry Brown	\$10.00	0-679-73491-0
Dirty Work by Larry Brown	\$9.95	0-679-73049-4
Harry and Catherine by Frederick Busch	\$10.00	0-679-73076-1
Sleeping in Flame by Jonathan Carroll	\$10.00	0-679-72777-9
Cathedral by Raymond Carver	\$10.00	0-679-72369-2
Fires by Raymond Carver	\$9.00	0-679-72239-4
No Heroics, Please by Raymond Carver	\$10.00	0-679-74007-4
Short Cuts by Raymond Carver	\$10.00	0-679-74864-4
What We Talk About When We Talk About Love by Raymond Carver	\$9.00	0-679-72305-6
Where I'm Calling From by Raymond Carver	\$12.00	0-679-72231-9
Will You Please Be Quiet, Please? by Raymond Carver	\$10.00	0-679-73569-0
The House on Mango Street by Sandra Cisneros	\$9.00	0-679-73477-5
Woman Hollering Creek by Sandra Cisneros	\$10.00	0-679-73856-8
I Look Divine by Christopher Coe	\$5.95	0-394-75995-8
Dancing Bear by James Crumley	\$10.00	0-394-72576-X

VINTAGE
CONTEMPORARIES

V I N T A G E
CONTEMPORARIES